MEET THE FORTUNES!

Fortune (?) of the Month: Nash (Fortune) Tremont

Age: 28

Vital Statistics: He's a cop by profession, but he looks more like a cowboy. From the top of his Stetson to his well-worn boots, Nash is strong and sexy...and he has a secret.

Claim to Fame: The Austin Fortunes have been trying to track him down for more than a year (he's another of Gerald Robinson's legendary offspring). Surprise! Nash is hiding in plain sight—and you won't believe what he's up to!

Romantic Prospects: Not interested. Nash is working on a case and can't afford distractions. And that's all Cassie Calloway is, right?

"Everyone told me that coming to Texas would be a mistake. But the clues in my case led right to Austin, and I wasn't about to leave any stone unturned. My plan is to get in and out of town as fast as possible—before anyone realizes who I am.

"I hate lying to Cassie. But my time here is limited. No sense in getting too close. No sense in taking her in my arms, or dreaming about her at night. Because none of it is real. It can't be. No matter how I feel when she looks at me..."

THE FORTUNES OF TEXAS: THE RULEBREAKERS—

Making their own rules for love in the Wild West!

Dear Reader,

Family has always been important to me and a recurring theme in my books. Maybe I like to explore family relationships because I'm an only child. However, I was fortunate to have many aunts, uncles and cousins nearby for most of my growing-up years.

The Fortunes of Texas family provides so many directions and relationships to explore. My hero Nash, a detective who is investigating the Fortunes, is quite happy with his small family of himself and his mom, who was abandoned by the love of her life—a Fortune. Nash wants nothing to do with the man who hurt his mother or the Fortunes' extended family. But when he meets Cassie, a cute, quirky artist and bed-and-breakfast owner, he begins thinking of family in a new way. Cassie awakens a kind of love he never experienced before.

I hope you enjoy Nash and Cassie's love story.

Best,

Karen Rose Smith

Fortune's
Family Secrets

Karen Rose Smith

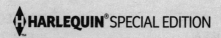

Special thanks and acknowledgment are given to Karen Rose Smith for her contribution to The Fortunes of Texas: The Rulebreakers continuity.

Recycling programs
for this product may
not exist in your area.

ISBN-13: 978-1-335-46566-5

Fortune's Family Secrets

Copyright © 2018 by Harlequin Books S.A.

HARLEQUIN®
www.Harlequin.com

Printed in U.S.A.

USA TODAY bestselling author **Karen Rose Smith** has written over ninety novels. Her passion is caring for her four rescued cats, and her hobbies are gardening, cooking and photography. An only child, Karen delved into books at an early age. Even though she escaped into story worlds, she had many cousins around her on weekends. Families are a strong theme in her novels. Find out more about Karen at karenrosesmith.com.

Books by Karen Rose Smith

Harlequin Special Edition

The Montana Mavericks: The Great Family Roundup

The Maverick's Snowbound Christmas

The Montana Mavericks: The Baby Bonanza

The Maverick's Holiday Surprise

Fortunes of Texas: All Fortune's Children

Fortune's Secret Husband

The Mommy Club

The Cowboy's Secret Baby
A Match Made by Baby
Wanted: A Real Family

Reunion Brides

Riley's Baby Boy
The CEO's Unexpected Proposal
Once Upon a Groom
His Daughter...Their Child

Montana Mavericks: Rust Creek Cowboys

Marrying Dr. Maverick

The Baby Experts

Twins Under His Tree
The Texan's Happily-Ever-After
The Texas Billionaire's Baby

Visit the Author Profile page
at Harlequin.com for more titles.

In memory of my dad, Angelo Jacob Cacciola, who taught by example that creativity could be expressed in painting, woodworking and model train platforms.

Chapter One

Nash Tremont came down the stairs from the second floor of the Bluebonnet Bed-and-Breakfast and followed the aroma of cinnamon and sugar and some kind of bread. His boots didn't make a sound on the steps. After all, he was a police detective and instincts died hard.

At the bottom of the staircase, he spotted a sight that suddenly made him hungry for more than cinnamon rolls. He'd hardly said two words to the proprietress of the bed-and-breakfast but now he couldn't stop himself. "Even a veteran cowgirl should know better than to climb a ladder that's too short."

Cassie Calloway squeaked as if he'd startled her. Her name was an easy one to remember, but he wasn't thinking about her name as she tilted on the ladder, almost losing her balance. He rushed to her side and wrapped his hands around her waist. It was a tiny waist but she was plenty curvy above and below it.

"Sorry," he said. "I didn't mean to startle you."

Gaining her footing once more, she peered down at him. Her tousled brown hair flowed forward and her dark brown eyes moved from his face to his hands at her waist. He quickly removed them, though they tingled because he'd felt her warmth underneath her blouse.

"What makes you think I'm a veteran cowgirl?" she asked, climbing down the ladder.

"Your boots," he answered quickly. He'd been trained to notice details.

She looked down at her boots as if she hadn't remembered what she was wearing. They were brown leather, well creased, with the shine long gone.

"They're comfortable and I like to cook in them." She sounded a bit defensive.

"I came down because something smelled wonderful. But if we keep up this conversation, I have a feeling you're not going to give me anything you made for breakfast."

She laughed and it was a pretty sound. When had he last noticed a woman's laughter?

On the ceramic tile of the kitchen floor now, Cassie Calloway looked up at him. She wasn't short, maybe about five-seven. But he was six-three so her chin had to come up for her to meet his eyes. "You didn't come down for breakfast yesterday. Didn't smell the bacon?"

Yesterday he'd still been trying to make sense out of what he was doing. Oh, he knew what his mission was here in Austin, Texas. Although he was the love child of an affair between his mother and Jerome Fortune, aka Gerald Robinson, he wasn't in Austin about that. He had no desire to see his biological father. He *was* after information—information that could land Gerald Robinson's wife, Charlotte, in jail. He hoped he didn't run into any of his half brothers or sisters, either. He didn't want anything to muddy his investigation or sway his judgment. He was undercover and intended to keep a low profile.

"Maybe I just like cinnamon more than bacon." Teasing Cassie and seeing her smile seemed to make his day. Maybe because everything about why he was here was so serious.

"I didn't know financial consultants were so picky," she joked back.

He almost winced. He'd needed a cover story. A financial consultant on vacation from Mississippi seemed the perfect one to hide his real identity: a detective from Mississippi investigating fraud.

When Cassie Calloway looked into his dark brown eyes with hers, he felt his conscience stab him. He wished he could tell her the truth. But that was ridiculous. He didn't even *know* this woman, let alone know if she was trustworthy. Hormones were the downfall of many a man and he'd do well to remember that.

He nodded to the ladder and the smoke alarm in the ceiling. "What's the problem?"

She opened her hand to reveal a new nine-volt battery. "I need to change the battery, but I couldn't quite reach it."

"And you shouldn't have tried. Don't you have a handyman's number you can call when you need one?"

She scoffed at that and shook her head. "Handyman? I don't think so. I have a mortgage and I need to fill rooms. That's why I opened them to extended stays. You're the first one to take advantage of that."

Nash looked around at the quirky colors of paint on the walls—lime green and sky blue—as well as a mural that had to have been hand-done. It depicted a scene of children sitting under a huge oak. A cowboy was seated on a stool with an open book in his lap as he read them a story. It was really good and he realized the bright wall colors complemented those in the painting.

"You have a nice place here. Have you done many renovations?"

She moved a few steps away from him as if the distance was necessary to talk to him. "I fell in love with it as soon as I saw it. It was in foreclosure. It mainly needed fresh coats of paint."

He nodded to the mural. "Who did your artwork?"

Her cheeks turned a little pink. "I did."

"You've got talent."

Her eyes were bright and her smile wide when she said, "Thank you. I love to paint. I mean *real* paintings. I was an art history major in college, and I took education courses so I could teach. But teaching positions are hard to find in these days of budget cuts, especially *art* teaching positions."

Glancing around again, taking in the whole bed-and-breakfast's first floor as if it was a piece of art, he decided, "You shouldn't let your talent go to waste."

"Oh, I don't. I teach private art lessons, and I help with the community art center." After a brief hesitation, she said, "Now that I told you about me, why don't you tell me about Mississippi?"

He knew she'd called his reference in Oklahoma, the state where he was born. Dave Preston was a close friend who could and would adhere to Nash's cover story.

Nash held his hand out for the battery. "Why don't you let me take care of this before you actually need the smoke alarm?"

"If you're sure you don't mind—"

Not minding a bit, he took the battery from her palm. The tips of his fingers touching her skin sent an electric jolt through him. No, no, no! He didn't have time for an attraction now. He had to save his energy for the job he was here to do and not be distracted by a pretty woman.

Climbing the ladder, he easily changed the battery. Then he was down the ladder once more.

She glanced down at his well-worn boots. "Your boots look comfortable, too."

He had to chuckle. "Yes, they are. Perfect for walking or driving."

"Not for meeting clients?"

Damn it. He was going to have to buy a new pair of boots so he could show her he dressed up for client meetings. Not that he had any of those planned.

He winked at her. "I prefer black boots for a more professional look."

She seemed to look him up and down, from his dark brown hair, over his squarish jaw, down his red T-shirt and his jeans. Her gaze on him made him feel hot.

"I clean up well, too."

She blushed. "Oh, I didn't think you didn't. How about that cinnamon roll?" she asked, obviously embarrassed.

"That sounds good. Join me?" The question came out of his mouth before he thought better of it. He really shouldn't have asked her that.

She hesitated and he thought that was wise of her. After all, even though she'd called his reference, he was practically a stranger. But then deciding it must be safe enough to have breakfast with him, she waved at the eat-at counter on the kitchen side of the room. The other side of the room was filled with tables and chairs, no doubt for the dinner he remembered she also served. He hadn't taken advantage of that yesterday simply because he didn't want to get tied up with her or any other guests. Anonymity was best cultivated if he spent most of his time alone. However, after a quick canvas of the comfortable-looking sitting area, he could see himself working on his laptop there.

"Coffee?" Cassie asked.

"If it's black and strong."

"It is," she said, but then smiled. "I dose mine with cream and sugar."

He rolled his eyes in mock horror. "None of those for me."

"At least I don't serve flavored coffees."

He laughed at her tone. "Your guests don't ask for a hazelnut latte or maybe a caramel macchiato?"

"How do you know about that, since you're a black-coffee drinker and all?"

Their gazes locked for a heartbeat. It was just one of those awareness moments that passed between a man and a woman when they felt chemistry. "I've been in a coffee shop or two."

She looked away first. "I've been known to make a flavored pot of coffee for my women guests. Most of the men are like you and just want theirs black."

Just like him? He doubted that.

More serious now, she asked, "Is there a reason you

didn't stop for breakfast yesterday? You just filled a travel mug with coffee and left."

He'd have to watch himself around her. She also seemed to pay attention to details. "I was in a hurry."

"And not today?"

"I have an appointment this morning but it's a little later." Another lie. Well, not exactly a lie. He did have an appointment to use a computer at the library. He had research to do, and it was going to take hours and hours if not days or weeks. But he'd find what he was looking for.

She motioned again to the stool at the eat-at counter. "Sit and I'll get your breakfast."

"I can put the ladder away for you first if you'd like."

She seemed to contemplate that for a few beats. "Okay. Let me show you where it goes."

He noticed that Cassie moved quickly and gracefully. He couldn't help but watch the gentle sway of her hips as she led him through the dining area. To the right, there was a screened-in porch. It might be nice to sit out there with his laptop, too. He wished he could just access the records he wanted on there, but he couldn't. He didn't want any research being traced back to him. He'd switch around from computer to computer at the library on different days. Once he found what he was looking for, he'd have to have it printed out. There again he didn't want to send emails to himself and have a record of it. His boss in Mississippi had been totally against this investigation because their original case there had been closed. But once Nash had found that Charlotte Robinson could have used the alias Charlene Pickett, he just couldn't let it go.

Following Cassie distracted him from the work he

intended to do. She was sexy in jeans and a boyfriend shirt. She'd rolled up the sleeves and left the collar open. All too well, he could imagine her in one of *his* shirts.

Putting the brakes on that image, he let her guide him down a hall.

She motioned to the left to a half-open door. "That's my suite."

Continuing down the hall, she opened another door on the left. He could see right away it was a utility room with a washer and dryer, a step stool and an open ironing board.

She pointed to the back of the room. "Can you just prop the ladder there for now?"

It was a tight fit sliding past the ironing board but he slanted the ladder against the wall. Cassie had slipped into the area with him, probably to make sure the ladder was securely propped. She acted like a woman who was used to being on her own and doing for herself.

Suddenly, though, they were face-to-face and boots to boots. His eyes locked to hers and he could again feel the thrum of chemistry between them. From the surprise in her eyes, he could see she felt it and recognized it, too. Attraction to Cassie Calloway was way too dangerous to even contemplate.

Again she broke eye contact first and retreated through the opening between the ironing board and the washer and dryer. "I really should close the ironing board," she said, her cheeks an attractive pink. "But I hate setting it back up every time I want to iron something."

"You iron things often?" He was amused by that thought, though he knew his mother was particular about her clothes, too. She'd even ironed pillowcases.

"I like to be presentable," she answered, a little defensively. "Besides, my guests often need to iron their clothes after traveling. They have sleeve boards in the closets in their rooms, but sometimes they're not adequate."

"I do have a couple of dress shirts I should iron," he decided.

"Do you have many clients in Austin?" she asked.

"Enough." He knew to keep personal answers short and concise.

Cassie waited, possibly to see if he'd tell her more, but he didn't. Her cheeks still pink, she said, "I'll get your breakfast ready. Would you like eggs with that cinnamon roll?"

She was already a good five feet ahead of him as she sped out of the utility room.

He called after her, "No eggs." Yet he might have *two* rolls…if they were good.

Cassie didn't know what it was about Nash Tremont that sent a tingle up her spine. She usually kept civility and politeness between her and men, especially those she might be attracted to. She had secrets. From experience, she knew she couldn't share them. That was just the way it was.

But as Nash sat on the stool watching her ready his breakfast, she felt nervous and a bit excited. As she carried two rolls to the counter, along with two mugs of coffee, she asked, "Are you originally from Oklahoma or Mississippi?"

Nash's brows arched. "You didn't ask Dave Preston that when you called for a reference?"

"He told you I called?"

"He did. We're good friends."

Taking a seat next to Nash, careful their elbows didn't brush, she pulled the sugar bowl over to her mug of coffee. "I learned that from our conversation. He told me you'd been friends for years, that you often helped him out with construction projects around his house, that you were good with his kids and his dog. He gave you an A-plus rating."

Nash laughed. "Maybe Dave wasn't used to giving references. He wanted to make sure he didn't miss anything."

"He acted as a friend should. Anyway, your accent isn't pure Mississippi, is it?"

Again Nash gave her a short answer. "I was born and raised in Oklahoma, and if you put too much sugar in that coffee, you're going to crash later today."

She'd been too busy looking at Nash's thick brown hair, and studying the jut of his jaw. She hadn't been paying attention to how many teaspoons of sugar she'd put in her coffee. She'd have to drink it no matter how sweet it was. "No, I don't crash. I just eat more sugar or drink more caffeine."

"Let's see," Nash said with mock seriousness. "Didn't your website say something about serving healthy breakfasts and dinners?"

"That's for my guests who want *healthy*. I eat when I can and usually on the go, especially when I do Paint and Sip presentations."

"Paint and Sip?" He looked perplexed.

"It's a recent wine trend. Local wineries have me in for a Paint and Sip night. I teach their customers how to paint a painting in one night while they sip wine."

"What a great marketing tool," he said.

"It is, and it brings in extra money." She always needed to do that. Her life had been that way since she was a child.

"How about you?" Nash asked. "Are you from Austin?"

Should she tell him? Why not? After all, he wasn't from around here. "I grew up not so far away."

The cinnamon rolls were round and she took hers apart, licking the sugar glaze off her fingers as she did. When she turned toward Nash, he was studying her.

"What?"

"Do you always eat your cinnamon rolls that way?"

Noticing his was gone with two big bites, well, maybe three, she shrugged. "I prolong the experience. Besides…aren't sweets better if you can lick them off your fingers?"

Something glowed in Nash Tremont's eyes and she wished she hadn't said that. There was coiled energy in the man and plenty of sensual energy, too.

As she felt tongue-tied, not knowing what else to say, he drank most of the coffee in his mug. Leaning back a degree, he gave her a smile that didn't reach his eyes. "Your cinnamon rolls are delicious and the coffee is just what I needed. If you don't mind, I'll take a travel mug full of it along with me again."

"I don't mind. Would you like another cinnamon roll for on the road?"

"Yes, I would," he agreed.

"I'll wrap one for you. Will you be here for dinner tonight?"

There was no hesitation in Nash's voice. "No, I won't. I'll be having dinner out." He'd brought his travel mug with him and now he filled it from the urn in the din-ing area. "Will more guests be checking in?"

Cassie had hopped up from her stool and was wrap-ping a second roll. "Yes. Thank goodness there will be another couple today. Do you like to mingle when you go out of town or take vacations?"

"I don't take many vacations."

"A workaholic?"

"Something like that," he acknowledged.

Going back to the counter he picked up the roll she'd wrapped in foil. Then he gathered his Stetson from one of the hat racks on the wall and took out his keys. "Thanks again for breakfast. I'll see you sometime." Then, without another word, he was gone.

Cassie had noticed how he avoided personal ques-tions and turned them around on her. She shrugged it off. Maybe Nash Tremont was just a very private man.

Nash gripped the steering wheel of his SUV tighter as he followed the car's GPS directions to the library. But even with that greater tactile stimulation of his hands, even though his thoughts should be perusing the dates of the archives he wanted to look up, he felt both-ered by what had happened at the bed-and-breakfast. He shook his left hand, then he put it back on the wheel and shook his right. Still he could feel a tingle in his fingers from the warmth of touching Cassie Calloway. It was absolutely crazy.

He hadn't even looked at a woman with real interest since Sara. His bitterness over what had happened with her had leveled off into disappointment. The divorce rate among cops was well above the average. He'd told himself that over and over again. He'd told himself that his work was enough.

Suddenly his dashboard lit up. A female computer voice told him, "Mom is calling."

He reached to the dash and pressed a button on the digital screen. "Hi, Mom." He'd called her when he'd reached Austin so she wouldn't worry.

"I thought I'd give you a call before we both got involved in our days."

He checked the time on the dash. "This is early for you, isn't it?" It was only 8 a.m.

"I'm going into work early today, lots of new car policies to write up. Must be spring. Drivers like to spruce up their cars or buy a new one."

Nash smiled. His mother worked for an insurance company that wrote car and homeowner policies. She'd been working there for years and seemed to enjoy it.

"How do you like Austin?" she asked.

It seemed like an idle question but he knew she was fishing. "You didn't tell anybody I was coming here, did you?"

"Who would I tell?" she asked innocently.

"If anyone calls from my office in Biloxi, you tell them I went camping in the backwoods, okay? And if Ben Fortune phones again, stick with the story that you don't know where I am." Some of his half siblings had tried to get in touch by mail and phone, but he'd ignored their requests.

Nash heard his mom let out a sigh. "I still don't understand why you can't be honest about what you're doing at work."

"Because I'm not supposed to be doing it." He'd told

her this before when he'd explained why he was spending time in Austin.

"This is on your own time. Why would anybody care?"

"There's a hierarchy. The chief told me to drop this, so he'd be very unhappy if he knew I didn't."

"I get that. Are you sure you don't want to look up your father while you're there?"

"I'm sure."

"I told you before, he's not as terrible as the media makes him sound."

His mother had her memories, but Nash knew the facts. Gerald Robinson had supposedly walked away from the Fortune money and built himself up from scratch. But he'd had many indiscretions along his road to success. Most of them had made their way into the media. Nash still couldn't believe his mother wasn't bitter about what had happened to her. Gerald had been married when he had an affair with Marybeth Tremont, but she'd had no expectations going into the affair. He'd given her that old line about his wife being a gold digger and not understanding him. But a man who cheated was a man who cheated. However, Gerald's indiscretions were the reason Nash had so many half brothers and sisters he'd never met.

His mother's voice came through the speaker again. "Is what you're doing dangerous?"

"No, it's not dangerous. I'm just rounding up background information and this is the best place to do it. With the Robinsons living here, I can nose around, listen to gossip, maybe even get close to them without anybody knowing who I am."

"I want you to be careful," his mother warned him.

"I'm always careful."

He thought he heard her snort before she said, "You know Oklahoma isn't quite as far from Austin as Biloxi is. If you wrap up early what you're doing, you can fly home and visit."

He didn't get home as often as he thought he should. But there were memories there he didn't want to revisit. Still, his mother was right. If he did wrap this up quickly, he should fly to Oklahoma for a visit.

"Let me see what happens here, Mom. I took a month of vacation."

"You know, when I tell you to be careful this time, my advice isn't simply about being careful physically."

"What are you worried about?"

"I'm worried if you do run into a half brother or sister, or your father, you'll leave Austin, stay removed from people who *are* your family and have many regrets. But I'm also worried that if you somehow make contact, you'll get hurt."

"I won't get hurt. I don't have any expectations. This is an investigation about wrongdoing…and fraud, Mom. That's it."

"If you say so."

His mother often used that phrase when she didn't agree with him. He knew it and she knew it.

"Are you going to stop for breakfast instead of just drinking coffee?" she asked.

She also knew him too well. "I actually did have breakfast this morning. The bed-and-breakfast served cinnamon rolls."

"And? How were they?"

"Cassie gave me one to bring along for a snack." He said the words without thinking, and the picture of her unwinding her cinnamon roll and licking the icing from her fingers made him almost break out in a sweat.

"Cassie?"

Uh-oh. He should have been watching his tongue. This investigation really did have him rattled. "She owns the bed-and-breakfast."

"Is she old and gray?"

Again, as if a photo flashed in front of his eyes, he saw Cassie's pretty face, her long brown wavy hair, her chocolate-brown eyes. "She's probably about my age, but do not make anything of it."

"Didn't you say the bed-and-breakfast offers breakfast and dinner?"

"It does if anyone signs up for it."

"You're a growing boy. Take advantage of it."

What his mother was really saying was that he should sit down for meals, get to know people and not isolate himself. Isolation not only kept his job safe but his heart, too. You couldn't spill something you weren't supposed to when you weren't around anyone to spill it to.

"I know you," she went on. "You'll do what you want to do in spite of what I say. But I love you anyway. I've got to go now or I'll be late. You take care and stay out of trouble."

His mother still spoke to him as if he were sixteen. But they'd been through his lifetime together, watching out for each other. He loved her dearly. "You have a good day, Mom. I'll let you know if I can come for a visit."

His mother ended the call. When he thought about their conversation, he remembered her advice.

Should he have dinner with Cassie tonight?

Chapter Two

Cassie was grateful when Trina and Joe Warner checked in. Sometimes guests didn't even bother to cancel their reservations when they weren't going to come, so she was never sure if a reservation would be kept. Not until her guests actually arrived.

Trina and Joe were in their early sixties, retired and on a road trip to visit family in Oklahoma. After check-in, they'd freshened up, then had come downstairs to join her as she cooked them dinner. Actually, she was cooking enough for four. It was possible that Nash might want to warm up something when he returned to the B&B.

Nash Tremont. She'd been thinking about him too much today...the way his brown hair dipped over his brow, the way his Stetson had set at just the right angle as he'd left this morning. What was it about the man that seemed to make her giddy?

The Warners had plenty to chat about and Cassie could easily see that many guests who stayed at a bed-and-breakfast enjoyed meeting people from different locales. She filled them in about Austin sites until dinner was ready. Tonight she'd cooked a beef-and-beans enchilada casserole along with cornbread biscuits and a salad.

She was pouring the Warners glasses of iced tea from an antique pitcher she'd found in a consignment shop when Nash came in. He frowned when he saw her and the couple at the table. Being the good hostess that she attempted to be, she was ready to acknowledge him when he raised his hand to her as if he wasn't going to stay, but rather go up to his room.

Her manners made her ask, "Are you sure you wouldn't like to join us? There's plenty. And I have chocolate cream pie for dessert."

The Warners waved at the casserole on the table. Joe was already scooping out a serving. "We watched her make it," he said. "Ground beef, chili powder, cumin, beans, chili peppers and sour cream. Tortillas in the bottom and the middle."

Nash's nose twitched as if it was catching the scent of dinner and it might intrigue him. He smiled at the couple, then Cassie, but Cassie thought it took an effort. She guessed he was going to refuse her offer of dinner.

However, he surprised her when he asked, "Did you say chocolate cream pie?"

Cassie laughed. "So the casserole won't do it but chocolate cream pie will?"

After a shrug, he gave her a boyish grin. "Like my

mama always says—I have a sweet tooth that just won't quit." He came over to the table and Cassie noticed again his no-nonsense stride, his confident posture, the twinkles she'd glimpsed in his eyes this morning. She made introductions. He took the chair at the side of the table where he could face the door.

Trina served herself a portion of the casserole and spooned a generous serving for Nash onto his plate. After he thanked her, he met Cassie's gaze. "It smells good. And I do like chilis."

After Cassie poured Nash a glass of iced tea, too, she took a seat next to Trina across from him. He'd taken off his Stetson and placed it on the sideboard. She didn't know if he knew how to ride, but she could easily imagine him on a horse. When she was a little girl, a school friend of hers lived on a ranch. Cassie escaped to Deborah's place as often as she could. Debbie had two parents who loved her, took care of her and cared about Cassie, too. She'd been grateful to have a motherly figure watching over her since her own mother hadn't been able to do it.

Silence reigned at the table as everyone dug into the portions on their plates or took a cornbread biscuit from the basket Cassie had lined with a napkin.

Joe slathered his biscuit with butter. "Delicious."

His wife nudged him. "You haven't even tasted it yet!"

"I can tell from its lightness." He took a bite. "Like I said—delicious."

Everyone at the table laughed.

"How long have you been married?" Nash asked.

"Forty years this summer," Trina answered.

Joe patted his wife's hand. "The best years of my life!"

Cassie swallowed hard. Was that kind of marriage even possible? She thought again about Debbie's parents. Yes, she supposed it was. She explained to Nash, "Joe and Trina stopped here on their way to Oklahoma. They're visiting family."

Nash's gaze met Cassie's and she knew why. He'd told her he was from Oklahoma. Maybe he didn't want her to bring it up. She, of course, wasn't going to spill his personal background.

"What part of Oklahoma?" Nash asked. "I was born and bred there."

"We're heading for Tulsa. Where did you live?"

"Oklahoma City. I was raised by my mom. She insists she did a good job. But I'm not sure how many people would agree with her."

Joe took another biscuit and chuckled. "If she's proud of you, that's all that matters."

As they ate, Nash asked leading questions of the Warners, and they delved into the subject of their children... and their grandchildren.

Cassie thought again that Nash knew how to deflect attention from himself. She noticed it because she knew how to do it, too. The people she'd come to know in Austin believed her parents were dead. She hadn't corrected them because she didn't want the truth to get out.

After coffee and chocolate cream pie, Cassie asked the Warners, "Will you be stepping out tonight?"

The husband and wife looked at each other and shook their heads. "No. We're going to enjoy our beautiful room and just watch some TV. Tomorrow, we'll go sightseeing to some of those places you mentioned."

Joe stood, patted his stomach, which protruded over his belt, and waited for his wife to stand, too. After good-nights all around, they crossed to the staircase and climbed the stairs.

"Nice couple," Nash said as Cassie started to clear the table.

It felt odd being alone with Nash…it seemed intimate in some way. That was silly. Yes, they were alone in her downstairs, but there was nothing intimate about it. Still, feeling self-conscious, she busied herself with clearing the table. To her surprise, Nash helped her and brought dirty dishes to the counter.

"You don't have to do that," she said. With him standing beside her, he seemed to take up all the space in the small kitchen.

"It's no bother. It's the least I can do after that good meal."

She decided to keep the conversation as light as she could. "A man raised with good manners is hard to find these days," she teased.

"Wow! That makes me wonder about the kind of men you date." With a brow arched, he leaned his hip against the counter, looking relaxed…and too sexy for words.

His comment was bait and she understood that. He was trying to find out something about her. "Date? I don't have time for dating," she explained, keeping her reason light and short.

"A busy life. I can certainly see *that*. I can't believe you run the B&B and still have time to take on art students…and volunteer somewhere. Let alone your winery nights."

Because of his comment, Cassie could tell he had

been thinking about what she'd told him. Why? "You have a good memory."

"Only when I'm interested."

He had to mean interested in the conversation, right? He wasn't even from Austin. He couldn't be interested in *her*.

Nash quickly opened the dishwasher and began loading the dishes inside. "I would help my mom with things around the house. I'm sure you did with your mom, too."

Cassie just nodded but didn't say anything else.

Nash gave her a sideways look.

Still, she kept silent. Too many memories of her taking care of the cooking and the dishes and everything else, while her mom drank herself into oblivion, played unbidden on her mental screen. Thoughts of her mother were frequent still. Her mother didn't want to see her or hear from her...not while she was in prison. Every day Cassie hoped that where her mother lived now, she might not have any choice but to find help and detox.

Her thoughts were cut off as Nash straightened and she realized how close they were standing to each other. She passed him a plate. His fingers brushed hers as he took it from her. There was heat...not only in her fingers. And when she looked up into his eyes, there seemed to be sparks there that ignited sparks in her. He was a guest. He'd be leaving at the end of April. She couldn't even think about sparks...and kissing—

Kissing? Where had *that* come from?

She turned away from him, picked up a dish towel and began wiping crumbs from the counter into her hand.

Nash asked lightly, "Anything else I can help with?" His deep voice seemed to affect her as much as his touch. But she wasn't a coward, so she turned to face him. "Nope. Nothing else."

Their gazes collided again for at least three heart-beats. Then he nodded and went to collect his hat that was still on the sideboard. He carried it with him to the stairway, but then he said to her, "Good night. Sleep well."

Before she could return the sentiment, he was up the stairs and gone. Had she imagined the chemistry between them?

Feeling as if she'd been caught in a whirlwind, she added detergent to the dishwasher and started it. She just needed a good night's sleep. That was all. She'd go to bed, close her eyes and forget all about Nash Tremont.

When Nash returned to the bed-and-breakfast the next day, it was almost lunchtime. He'd taken the morn-ing off from doing research to drive around Austin to check out where the Fortunes' and Robinsons' influence could be seen. He'd also gotten a better handle on the city—the neighborhoods and the housing divisions. He had even driven around the college. Midmorning he'd found a leather goods shop and bought himself a pair of black dress boots. He'd also stopped at a men's store and purchased a sports jacket. That way, if he wanted to give Cassie the impression he was meeting a client, he'd fit the part better.

The part. He didn't know why it bothered him to play a part with Cassie, but it did.

The front door to the B&B was open and the screen door was allowing the spring air to flow in. As soon as Nash stepped inside, he heard a child's laughter. He liked kids. His old friend in Oklahoma—the one who had given Cassie a good reference—had three. He'd been to barbecues and Super Bowl parties with some of the guys at work. They had kids, too. Sometimes Nash liked the children even better than the adults.

Following the sound of childish chatter, as well as Cassie's voice, he crossed the dining area and passed the kitchen to the screened-in porch. There was an easel set up there with a chair in front of it. Cassie was sitting on a second chair beside a little girl who looked to be about eight. The girl's blond braids swung every time she turned toward Cassie.

Apparently hearing him approach the sliding glass door that was open today, Cassie spotted him peering through the screen. "Hi!" she said. "You're back."

Opening the screen and stepping inside the porch, he answered her. "Just for a little while. Then I'll be going out again. You're giving an art lesson?"

She motioned him to come farther inside.

He didn't move. "I don't want to interrupt."

"You're not," she assured him.

As he crossed to the area where Cassie and the child sat, the little girl turned around to face him. He noticed a child-sized cane propped against the wall. He raised questioning eyes to Cassie.

"Lydia, I want you to meet Nash. He's one of my guests here. Nash, this is Lydia."

"Hi, Lydia," he said easily. "Do you mind if I look at your painting?"

She gave a shy shrug and a smile, so he took that as a *yes*. Leaning down, he studied the picture of a Ferris wheel that was painted in bright colors and drawn with enough detail that he could see each seat. She'd painted people in the seats and she'd done a fairly good job of it, mostly drawing profiles. He wasn't sure he could do half as well.

"You have a terrific painting there. Did you ride on a Ferris wheel?" he asked.

This time Lydia grinned. "Mommy and Daddy took me to a carnival. I rode a pony, too."

"We're going to save horses for the next art lesson," Cassie confided. To Nash, she asked, "Have you eaten lunch?"

"Not yet."

"There are leftovers in the fridge."

"I'm going out again," he explained, ad-libbing.

"If you need a snack later, there's plenty. I didn't know if the Warners might be coming back for lunch and I wanted to provide something if they did." She frowned. "I had another cancellation."

With that declaration, Cassie looked and sounded worried.

Lydia had begun painting again, as if their conversation was of no consequence to her. He asked the little girl, "Do you mind if I sit and watch for a while?"

"I don't mind," she said. "I guess you wonder why I'm not in school today."

"The thought crossed my mind."

"My teachers had a meeting. Mommy had to work this morning. Cassie said she could give me a lesson, so Mommy's going to pick me up in a little while."

"You're lucky you could do this today."

"Yes, I am," Lydia agreed, bobbing her head and making her braids fly again.

Cassie suggested, "If you paint a fence around the Ferris wheel, it will ground it. Anybody looking at the painting will be able to tell the difference from the ground to the tippy top of the Ferris wheel."

Lydia nodded and went at it. "I'm going to mix two colors of brown for the fence."

Cassie squirted sienna and burnt umber on the palette. "See if you like those."

Fascinated by the process—and Cassie—Nash watched for the next half hour. Cassie was so patient with Lydia. Finally, he returned to the subject that seemed to have Cassie worried. He asked in a low voice, "Will it be a problem for you with another guest canceling?"

"I think I can make up the difference this month with the Paint and Sip party…if it's well attended. I have one coming up at the Mendoza Winery."

The winery was one of the Austin landmarks he'd noted. "I saw it today when I was driving around Austin."

He had driven around the Mendoza vineyard with its large acreage of grapevines. He'd discovered the winery had two offices—a small one at the edge of the vineyard and a larger corporate headquarters with its distribution center in Austin proper. Nash remembered he'd read somewhere that the winery had originally been named Hummingbird Ridge.

In spite of himself, he could imagine going to the tasting room with Cassie and sipping wine with her. He shook his head to erase the pictures from his mind. An attraction to her shouldn't even be an issue right now. He wasn't sitting that close to her because Lydia was between them. But he thought he could catch the scent of a flowery perfume. And Cassie's hair was so bright and shiny…and soft-looking. When she smiled, she had dimples. And there were freckles running across both of her cheeks. She was a tempting woman in so many ways. So many ways he was going to ignore.

Finally, Lydia was finished with her painting.

"Is she using acrylics?" Nash asked.

"They're so much easier for the children. As they become true artists, though, they can't mix them as well as they could oil paints. Some want to try watercolors, but using watercolors is its own art form—from the way you use the water to the texture of the paper."

"I can understand," Nash said, because he could. "More elements to deal with from the water spreading, the way the paper absorbs it, to the thinness of the brush."

The doorbell ringing suddenly interrupted their conversation. Lydia hopped up from her chair with her painting in hand. "I bet that's Mommy."

"I bet it is, too. Be careful with your painting."

Cassie opened the sliding screen door for Lydia. The little girl grabbed her cane and, as fast as she could, went to greet her mom.

"Why is she using a cane?" Nash whispered close to Cassie's ear. It *was* her shampoo he was smelling. And as his jaw brushed the side of her hair, he realized it was as soft as he imagined. Thoughts about kissing her were getting harder and harder to push away.

"She was in an accident riding her bike. She wasn't supposed to go onto a main street, but she did. A car sideswiped her. Fortunately, she was wearing a helmet and knee guards. That was three months ago. And she's just getting back on her feet. Her mom started bringing her to art lessons right after the accident. Lydia needed an outlet for all of her energy. Her mother had taken no-

tice of her drawings at school, and she thought it would
be a good idea. And it was. She's talented."

"It's bad enough when adults have to deal with dis-
abilities, but kids—" Nash shook his head.

As Cassie gazed into his eyes, he felt that connection
with her again. It was hard to believe he'd only known
her a few days, yet his pulse was beating fast.

Quickly, she turned away from him, took a few
steps back and said, "I have to say goodbye to Lydia's
mother."

In case Cassie had something private to say to Lydia's
mother or vice versa, Nash stayed on the porch, waiting for Cassie. When she returned there to clean up the
paints, Nash said, "Will you show me *your* paintings?"

She hesitated for a few moments. "I suppose I can.
The attic is my studio. It would have been too difficult
to make it into another bedroom for the B&B. But it *is*
the perfect place for a studio. Come on. I'll show you."

As Nash followed Cassie up the staircase, he wasn't
sure exactly *why* he wanted to see her paintings. Maybe
because he thought they'd give him a glimpse into who
she really was. Was she as sweet and caring as she
seemed? Or was it an act because she was the hostess
of the bed-and-breakfast? Hard to say. But he was an
investigator, so he was going to investigate.

Cassie ran up the stairs ahead of him. When she
reached the second floor, she waved down the hall and
pointed to the rope that hung from the ceiling. She
reached up and grabbed it and pulled down a staircase. The steps were narrow.

Nash commented, "This isn't exactly ideal working
conditions if you want to carry paintings up and down."

"Do you know any situation that's really ideal?"

Cassie asked as if she'd had a lot of experience dealing with curveballs life threw at her.

He knew exactly what she meant. People had expectations and what they envisioned rarely came to pass. At least, not without some adjustment.

Cassie wasn't as naive as he'd first thought she might be. It took years and life experience to know that nothing was perfect, that you couldn't wait around for it to *be* perfect. Just like his relationship with Sara. He hadn't realized until too late that it was never going to work… that in fact it was a lost cause.

After he'd climbed the stairs behind Cassie, Nash glanced around the attic. Light streamed in windows from both sides. Cassie had an easel set up with a drop cloth underneath much as she had downstairs on the porch. Only this easel was taller and wider, and it had a half-finished painting propped on it.

Before Nash studied that painting, he looked around at the others propped against the walls. The canvases were lined up, some overlapping. The colors were very much like the ones Cassie had chosen to use in the house. They were vibrant, with hot pinks and yellows and lime green, teal and even orange. And with those colors she'd captured her subjects beautifully—a hummingbird at a feeder, bluebonnets in a field with a child sitting with her back to the viewer, her blond hair blowing in the wind. Another one showcased an abstract cat, black and white against a sky-blue background. She'd also painted buildings that were a little more muted, a red barn and corral, a ramshackle house sitting in the woods, a blackbird sitting on a white fence. He could tell she was practicing styles, trying to find her own. Finally, his gaze fell to the canvas on the easel. This one was different from the others. Done mostly in pastels, it depicted an angel hovering over a child who was sitting on the grass reading a book. If it was up to Nash, he'd say that was her best work yet.

"How long did it take you to do these?" The creative process really did interest him.

"The past two years," she said. "I sell them when I can. Art shows are the best, but I often don't have time to give up a whole weekend for that."

"You're talented." It wasn't idle flattery. He meant it.

"Talent doesn't always pay the bills," she said, obviously being realistic about it. That was probably why she wanted to teach—for the consistent income.

Cassie was standing in front of the easel and he crossed to stand beside her. "I think that's the best one."

Her eyes widened in surprise. "Not the barn or the landscape outside of Austin?"

"Those are good," he conceded. "And if I had a den I'd probably hang them there. But aren't paintings supposed to evoke emotions?"

She pushed her hair away from her brow. "I'm surprised you know that."

"Because I'm a financial consultant?" he teased.

She shrugged. "Something like that. I mean, most people don't even know that that's why they choose a particular painting. I think art customers buy the paintings they do because that particular work resurrects a memory or a feeling they once had…or a feeling they want to have now."

Again, Nash was surprised at her insight.

"What?" she asked when she saw him studying her.

"You just surprise me, that's all."

They were standing very close now, facing each

other. He could easily reach out and touch one of the waves of her hair that flowed near her cheek. He was so tempted to lean in a bit to see what she would do. But he knew he was playing with fire. He knew he was being foolish, and she must have known it, too.

Suddenly she took a step back.

But he wouldn't let her escape just yet. "Are you sorry you brought me up here?"

"No, not sorry..." she trailed off, her voice a bit breathless.

He felt as if Cassie and her paintings had taken his breath away. "What then?"

In the afternoon light glowing through the window behind her, she looked vulnerable. "I don't often show my work to just anybody."

"You mean to a relative stranger?" he countered.

"Exactly."

A knowing came to him so swiftly that words came out of his mouth that he didn't expect. "After a few more days, I won't be a stranger, will I?"

"Maybe not," she murmured, then took another step back. "I have to make a grocery run and then prepare something for supper."

"And I have a meeting," he said, deciding if he was a financial consultant, he should meet with a client or two or three. After all, he now had boots to wear with a Western-cut jacket.

He motioned toward the stairs. "After you."

Once they were both on the second floor again and the stairs had been raised into the ceiling, he said, "So... I'll see you later. I have a few things I have to bring in from my SUV." He headed off down the hall, grateful he'd found a way to exit.

Because he'd almost done exactly what he knew he shouldn't. He'd almost kissed her.

Cassie was in the kitchen making a list of the groceries she'd need, trying not to think of her time with Nash in the attic. Just what had *that* been about? She'd felt such a pull toward him. He'd even seemed to understand her paintings. Unless that was an act…unless he was a player.

However, she didn't think so. She wasn't getting that vibe from him at all. Still, what did she know? It wasn't as if she had dated very much.

Almost finished with her list, she heard Nash's boots on the stairs. When he reached the first floor she glanced up and her heart beat in double time. He was wearing a Western-cut suit jacket, black dress jeans, white shirt and bolo tie. In his hands, he held his Stetson. He looked fantastic.

He turned toward her and smiled. "I thought you'd be out the door."

Because she'd run away from him so fast? She waved to the list on the counter. "I need to make sure I have everything written down that I need so I don't forget anything. Trips to the grocery store take too much time, and I don't want to be running there more than I have to."

"So you believe in efficiency? So do I."

She must have still been staring at him because he asked with a grin, "Do I have shaving cream on my nose?"

She felt herself blushing. "No. Of course not. What restaurant are you going to?"

She definitely thought he was meeting someone for

lunch. "I'm going to meet my client at his hotel and we'll go from there. Do you have any suggestions?"

"There's the Sundance Restaurant. Lots of business folk go there."

"I'll take that as a recommendation."

"Is there anything special you'd like me to pick up at the grocery store, maybe for snacks?"

"Corn chips and salsa," he responded with a wink.

"Mild or spicy?" she asked and then wondered if he thought that was a double entendre.

He must have because something sparked in his dark brown eyes. Something that made tingles dance on all her nerve endings.

"Definitely spicy," he answered.

"Got it." She definitely did. They were attracted to each other. Big-time.

He took his keys from his pocket and gave her a wave. "Have a good afternoon."

She said goodbye but wasn't sure he heard it because the door was already closing behind him.

She felt hot. How could a little conversation with a man make her feel hot? How could standing close to a man urge her to feel his kiss? How did looking at a man make her wish for so many things she couldn't have?

It was simple, really. A man like Nash wouldn't flirt with her at all if he knew her mother was in jail.

Chapter Three

Nash sat in a chair at a computer in the library forgetting all sense of time and place. The text on the screen, as well as the notes he had made, caused a sinking sensation in his stomach. He actually felt sick. Research on Jerome Fortune or Gerald Robinson, however you wanted to look at it, was not a feel-good experience.

In a normal investigation, he could contact the Robinsons for more information. But because he was investigating Gerald's wife, he couldn't do that.

Nash thought about his mother again and her lack of bitterness against Gerald. She must have really loved the guy. She'd told Nash that Gerald was lonely and his wife was a witch. As far as Nash was concerned, it was that old "she doesn't understand me" line. But if Charlotte Robinson was guilty of the crimes Nash suspected she was guilty of, maybe she really had been a witch…and still was.

Putting his notes aside, he stopped reading about the Robinsons in order to focus on photos. Gerald and Charlotte were in the paper constantly at charity fund-raisers, community events, when a new illegitimate child made the news. Nash didn't want the spotlight turned on himself. He definitely didn't intend to make the news.

He studied his father's face, unsure of what he was looking for. Signs of recognition? Was he trying to see himself in his father's face? He certainly hoped he couldn't find his own. He'd rather think he inherited all of his mother's attributes and physical features. But there was that hint of stubbornness in Gerald's jaw that Nash knew he had to own up to also.

He continued to pore over photo after photo. More recent ones caught his attention. He found the Fortune name mentioned in conjunction with a Valentine's Day party at the Mendoza Winery. Cassie had mentioned that winery and the fact she'd be doing a Paint and Sip party there.

If she taught her Paint and Sip class there, he could tag along or stop in incognito. It would be the perfect opportunity to nose around. Certainly, someone at the winery would remember the Valentine's Day party and the people who had attended. He could just claim he was thinking about contacting the famous family to in-quire if they needed his financial services. He had to keep his investigation moving forward. He didn't have that much time in Austin.

Wanting to ditch the suit he'd worn to his pretend meeting, he stuffed the small spiral-bound notebook with thoughts and facts about the Fortunes into an inside pocket. Then he closed down the computer. To his surprise, the afternoon had passed into evening. Immersed in his research, wondering how he could really get the goods on Charlotte, he'd lost track of time.

Rush-hour traffic was heavy as he headed back to the B&B. He found himself eager to see Cassie. She was like a bright star floating in and out of his mind, even as he tried to concentrate on grittier things like the Fortunes.

Fortunately, he found a parking space near the B&B. As he walked up the street, he thought again about the Paint and Sip party. The more he thought about going along with Cassie, the more he liked the idea. He was passing the house next door to the B&B when he realized someone was sitting on the porch in a caned rocking chair. The woman looked to be in her late sixties. She waved to him in a friendly greeting.

"Nice night," she called out. "But it's getting a bit chilly."

At the foot of the stairs to her porch, he stopped. "Yes, it is. Are you people-watching?" he asked with a smile.

"That's mostly what I do now," she said. "Especially in the evenings. I have a lot to watch with the B&B next door. I can see folks coming and going. I spotted you leaving earlier."

This woman must not have much to take up her time, and maybe not enough people in her life, Nash surmised. He went up the porch steps and extended his hand to her. "Nash Tremont," he said.

"I'm Renata Garcia."

"I'm enjoying the bed-and-breakfast. It's a nice atmosphere."

"Oh, yes, it is. Don't you just love the way Cassie painted those rooms? She has such a unique sense of style. Have you seen her paintings? She brought a few over after she moved in so I could see them. They're wonderful."

"She's very talented," Nash said noncommittally though he had really liked them. Apparently Cassie and this woman were friends.

"She is that, and she's such a lovely girl. She's helped me more than once when I wasn't feeling well. Some days my arthritis bothers me so much I can hardly get up and down out of the chair. But Cassie tells me to keep my cell phone close at hand and just call her if I need anything. In a way, I feel like a surrogate parent."

Nash knew he should get information about Cassie from Cassie herself, but he also realized he could learn facts from other people, too. "Aren't Cassie's parents around here?"

"It's such a shame, but Cassie's parents died in a car crash."

So Cassie had lost her parents. He felt for her. The compassion he'd seen in her was true. Apparently she knew what it was like to lose the people you loved.

He thought again about Sara and her refusal to marry him. She'd hurt his pride as well as broken his heart. Although he didn't intend to compare Sara and Cassie, he found himself doing it. Cassie seemed so bright and sparkling compared to Sara. Was it even fair to judge?

Cassie's neighbor broke into Nash's thoughts. "How long will you be staying at the Bluebonnet?"

"I'm not exactly sure," he told her. "More than a week and less than a month."

"I see. You know, you really should make a commitment. It would help Cassie figure out what bills she could pay and which ones she can't. She finagles her budget until it all works out. That's hard to do these days for me, too."

"I think we all have to adjust our budgets each month these days." He took off his sports jacket and laid it over his arm and then loosened his bolo tie. He couldn't wait to get into his T-shirt and jeans. "It was good to meet you, Renata."

"It was good meeting you, too. You tell Cassie I said hello."

"I'll be sure to do that."

As he descended the porch steps, he didn't know if he'd be seeing Cassie tonight. In some ways, it would be safer if he didn't. No temptation, no consequences. Maybe he'd change and go out again, grab some tacos and go over his notes. It would be a safe evening with nothing more on his mind than work.

The following day Cassie wished she could make a breakthrough with her eleven-year-old art student Danny. Art often could help children express themselves. She knew Danny could draw. That was one of the reasons his mother was paying for art lessons. But he wouldn't draw anything he really cared about.

The late afternoon was quiet on the porch as Cassie watched Danny paint the big sturdy tree, a realistic portrayal of one right outside the screened-in room. The only sound was the brush of Danny's strokes on the canvas and the sound of birds in the tree branches as they called to each other.

The almost-silence was the reason Cassie heard the front door open and then close. When she leaned back to peek through the rooms, she spotted Nash walking toward her. She hadn't seen him much for the last twenty-four hours. He hadn't eaten supper last night or breakfast this morning. He was dressed up again and he looked tired. Had he had meetings all day?

When he stopped at the door to the screened-in porch, Cassie motioned him inside. Maybe Danny would respond to another male.

"Danny, this is Nash. He's a guest at the bed-and-breakfast, and he understands paintings."

Danny gave her a quick glance and then turned back to his canvas.

"I really do," Nash said, obviously perceptive about what Cassie wanted him to do. "And Cassie's paintings are great. Have you seen any of them?"

Danny nodded but wouldn't turn and meet Nash's gaze. Nash lifted one eyebrow as if to ask Cassie what was going on. But she wouldn't talk about Danny with the boy there. Nash must have sensed that so he backed off, which was thoughtful of him.

He asked, "Is it okay if I make some coffee?"

She motioned to the sideboard in the dining area. "I brewed a pot about an hour ago. It should still be good. I made chocolate chip cookies, too. Danny had two before we started."

"What did you think of them?" Nash asked the boy.

"They were good," Danny answered, still keeping his eyes on the canvas.

But Nash didn't completely give up. "You know your tree is as good as any one of Cassie's."

Danny inclined his head as if he'd heard. He gave a little shrug, but he didn't respond. Nash's gaze locked with Cassie's, and he just pointed toward the dining room as if telling her he'd wait in there to talk with her.

A short time later, Danny's mother came in the door. Dorie Lindstrom always seemed to be in a rush. Now she came barreling toward the sunporch. Danny had his mom's blond hair and blue eyes, and when he saw her, he smiled. He always smiled around his mom.

As usual, she seemed to stop rushing when she was in the presence of her son. She stood behind him and stared at his painting. "That's a terrific tree. What are you going to put with it?"

"Maybe a playhouse on the grass," he said.

"You're good at painting buildings. I think that will fit well there, don't you think, Cassie?"

"Danny has an instinct for knowing what to fit together. I'm sure a playhouse will be just right."

Dorie handed Cassie a check. "Same time on Monday?"

"That works for me." As Danny rose to his feet, Cassie said, "I'll put your painting somewhere safe. It will be ready for you when you're ready for it." She placed her hand on his shoulder. "Good job."

He gave her a smile like he'd given his mom. Then the two of them left.

Cassie carefully propped the painting on one of the chairs, then collapsed the easel. By then Nash had come into the porch, coffee mug in hand. He'd removed his jacket and loosened his bolo tie. With the top button of his shirt opened, he looked too sexy for words. She swallowed hard and told herself again he was just a guest.

"So what's going on with your art student?" he asked. "Or can't you tell me?"

"Some things are confidential but it might help me to talk to you about it. I know you're not going to spread any gossip because you're not from here."

"That's right. No gossip passes my lips."

At the word *lips*, she stared at him...and them. That was a big mistake. She forced herself to concentrate on the subject they were talking about—Danny. "Danny's parents are going through a divorce."

"I see. Is he mad at his father? Is that why he wouldn't make eye contact with me? All males are taboo?"

How perceptive, Cassie thought. But she supposed Nash had learned to read his clients well. "That could be part of the reason. But even more than that, his father doesn't approve of Danny's interest in art. Danny's embarrassed about it himself because he's gotten teased at school. I'm trying to build his confidence along with teaching him about acclaimed male painters. I want him to know his talent is something to be proud of."

"You're right, it is. What kind of person is his father?"

"I haven't met him. He and his wife were separated before Danny started taking lessons. But he's a lawyer. From what Dorie says, I get the feeling he's narrow-minded in his thinking."

"And probably judgmental," Nash commented. "Narrow-minded people usually are."

"There are always two sides to every story, so I don't want to judge him without even meeting him. But from what Dorie has told me, both are true."

Nash leaned against the porch wall. "Do you know her well?"

"Not extremely well. She and I had a long conversation before I took Danny on. And we usually talk a little bit every time she picks him up. But today she must have been in an exceptional hurry. She seems to be a caring and attentive mom. She listens and he's completely relaxed when he's around her."

"And he probably wouldn't be that way with his dad," Nash guessed.

"Probably not. His dad wanted Danny to play football. That's not in the cards. I get the feeling that their differing views on raising children is one of the reasons the two of them broke up."

After another swallow of coffee, Nash said, "For what it's worth, I think you're doing the right thing building up his confidence. If he has confidence about his art, he'll have confidence in other areas."

Again, she was struck by his keen insight. She looked at him more closely. His hair was thick and a bit ruffled as if he'd run his fingers through it. He was a handsome man, that was for sure. "How did you get so wise?"

"The school of hard knocks."

She was thinking maybe Nash had had some counseling, but he'd just disabused her of that notion. Experience must have taught him everything he'd learned. She was eager to know what those experiences had been.

"Danny seems to be relaxed with you," Nash pointed out. "He wouldn't be able to concentrate on his painting if he wasn't. But then, I think anybody could be relaxed with you."

That compliment took Cassie by surprise. Truth be told, she wasn't used to receiving compliments from men. She'd dated back in Bryan before she'd decided to move her life to Austin. But once Cody Sinclair had found out her mother was in jail, he was out the door. Either his moral sensibilities had been offended or the idea of having a girlfriend whose mother was a felon was just too embarrassing or abhorrent. Cassie had known better than to get involved with anyone romantically after that if she didn't want a broken heart. Apparently romance just wasn't in the cards for her.

"How can you judge how relaxed people are with me?" she asked him. "You've only seen me with the Warners, Lydia and Danny."

"I had a talk with your neighbor yesterday when I came home. She was sitting on her porch and she waved and said hello."

"Mrs. Garcia is lonely," Cassie explained. "She's a widow."

"She said you spend time with her." His voice had gone gentle as if he appreciated that fact about her.

"I do. She's a lovely woman and has some great stories to tell. I think she's trying to keep her memories alive. She says when you reach a certain age, all of your memories tend to blur together. I enjoy spending time with her." Since her own mother wasn't in her life now—her mother's choosing, not hers—Renata Garcia helped fill a hole in her heart.

"She told me that you'd lost both your parents. I'm sorry to hear that."

Cassie was dumbfounded for a moment but maybe not entirely surprised that Renata had told Nash. Most of her neighbors and coworkers thought that was what had happened to her parents. The problem was—it was a lie. Somehow, making up a story for other people hadn't seemed so bad. She'd done it to protect herself and her mother and her business at the Bluebonnet. She'd seen everyone's reaction to Carol Calloway's arrest, trial and imprisonment. She'd learned it was better to propagate a myth and she'd had to do that to start over.

But Cassie felt terrible about lying to Nash. Still, hadn't her experience told her that was the best thing to do?

She decided it would be better to lead the subject away from herself. Since Nash *did* look tired, she asked, "How was your day?"

"Long," he answered with half a smile.

"Did you meet with potential clients? Did you sign any?"

Nash's brown eyes seemed to darken. His mouth turned down as if he was chagrined at her question.

She hurried to say, "I didn't mean to pry."

After a moment he explained, "Sometimes I learn information about my clients that I'd rather not know."

"I imagine a financial advisor's relationship with clients is somewhat like a lawyer's."

"I suppose they could be compared," Nash said politely, maybe a little coolly as if he didn't intend to talk about it anymore. He straightened, lifted his coffee mug to his lips and drained it. "Good coffee," he said. "I'll just set this in the sink."

"Will you be eating supper with us tonight?"

"No, I had a big lunch."

"There are sandwich fixings in the refrigerator if you find you want something later. Tomorrow night I'll be making a very early supper here. It's Paint and Sip night at the Mendoza Winery. If you want to get to know more about Austin, you could stop in. It's usually a friendly crowd."

"You've done this there before?"

"Two months ago. It went over really well, so we planned another one."

"I'll definitely consider it," he told her. "You have a good night."

Cassie followed him into the guest area and watched him put the mug in the sink. Then he picked up his jacket from the back of a chair and headed upstairs without looking back.

Maybe she'd been all wrong about an attraction between them. Maybe only *she* was the one who felt the attraction. Maybe she'd poked and prodded too much. Whatever the reason, she felt a bit rebuffed. She'd just keep her distance from Nash Tremont, and the attraction would go away on its own.

If Cassie had the opportunity and the funds, she'd eat at La Viña, the Mendoza Winery's restaurant, as often as she could. She liked the atmosphere there. The interior had a lot of large windows that during the day provided an extensive view of the vineyard. At night, floodlights showed off the grounds. The ceiling was oak-paneled and rounded to reflect the shape of the inside of a wine barrel.

The restaurant had been rearranged for the Paint and Sip party. Easels were set up along two sides of the restaurant. Patrons could pay the entire fee and actually paint a canvas with Cassie, or they could opt for a lesser fee that would cover only hors d'oeuvres and wine. That way friends who didn't want to paint could come along with friends who did. There were always a lot of watchers.

Carlo Mendoza had greeted Cassie and made sure she had everything she needed. His fiancée, Schuyler, acted as a hostess of sorts. Already this evening, Cassie had taken her students through a step-by-step process. They could wander around and study her painting. They could listen in as she migrated from student to student, giving help where needed. Servers poured wine and served plates of hors d'oeuvres as patrons went to the tables to enjoy conversation, wine and everything from crab balls to mini tacos.

Cassie was helping one of her students, a woman who had been to her last Paint and Sip party here, when she glanced around the room and spotted Nash. He hadn't told her he was coming. Of course, he didn't have to. Was he interested in actually painting? Or did he just want to try the Mendoza wines?

When she and her student finished their conversation, she moved on and noticed Nash was talking to Carlo. They seemed to be having a detailed conversation. She kept her eye on him as she walked around the room. When he'd finished speaking with Carlo, he crossed to a server who was headed toward the kitchen. They had a conversation, too. She wandered what that was all about.

Nash was dressed in an Oxford shirt and black jeans rather than a business suit. Still, was he making contacts?

The next time Cassie looked up to see where Nash had gone, he'd disappeared. Apparently, he wasn't staying for the evening.

After the customers had finished their paintings, the

restaurant emptied quickly. She packed her car, then went to find Carlo.

He came from the kitchen and spotted her. "I have your check," he said.

He handed her her portion of the proceeds for the evening. It was a nice chunk of money and would pay many of the bills that had started to pile up.

"Thanks for letting me do this again," she told him.

"No problem. It's beneficial for you and for me. We draw tourists as well as residents. And all of them can spread the word about our restaurant and wines as well as your bed-and-breakfast. Win-win."

Carlo Mendoza was a handsome man. He was over six feet tall, with dark hair and dark eyes, and very white teeth against a tan complexion. He could have been an actor or a model. He was a charismatic guy and before he fell for Schuyler, the word around town was that he'd had trouble with commitment. But whenever he and Schuyler were together, everyone knew that wasn't the case anymore.

Carlo had always been friendly, and now she hoped he wouldn't mind a question. "I spotted you speaking to one of my guests from the bed-and-breakfast earlier."

"Who was that?"

"His name is Nash Tremont."

"Oh, yes. He told me he's a financial advisor and making connections with clients while he's in town. He did tell me he was staying with you."

"I'm accepting guests for extended stays now. He was the first to sign up for one."

Carlo had a twinkle in his eye when he asked, "Are you interested in this guest?"

"Oh, no," Cassie assured him quickly. "He's from

Mississippi and he'll be returning there. There wouldn't be any point in me being interested."

Carlo gave a chuckle. "That depends on how interested you are."

Cassie felt herself blushing, and she knew exactly what Carlo meant. She could have a fling if she wanted, but that wasn't in her DNA. She shook her head again. "I know Nash has meetings planned while he's here. I guess he was asking you for leads?"

"Yes, he was. Especially information about the Fortunes. He'd seen photos online that some of them were here for the Valentine's Day party."

"I see," Cassie said, but she didn't really. Then again, she figured if you're in a town that wasn't your own, and there were famous, wealthy families in that town, you'd try to contact them.

That thought kept playing in her head during her drive back to the Bluebonnet. From what she'd seen of Nash thus far, he had good public relations skills. She imagined he was successful at what he did.

She was carrying paints and canvases to the porch when the subject of her thoughts asked, "Can I help you with that?"

Nash didn't wait for her to answer but took the toolbox-like carrier filled with paints out of her hand. They went up the porch steps together and he let her precede him inside.

She propped her painting against the counter and he set her paints beside it. Glancing at the sitting area, she could see a hassock was pushed away from an armchair, and there was a laptop on it.

"You were working there tonight," she said, and she wasn't sure why.

"Yes, I was. Do you need help bringing more supplies in from your car?"

She wouldn't turn down help when it was offered. "Sure. There's a stack of palettes and another box of paints. Would you like a glass of iced tea? I'm sure I can find cookies to go with it."

"No cookies," he said with a smile. "I had hors d'oeuvres at the Paint and Sip. But the iced tea would be great."

After he brought in the rest of her supplies, he asked, "Where would you like these?"

"There's a storage closet down the hall next to my room. If you could just set them in there, I'll take care of them later."

After he did that, Nash came back to the kitchen. Cassie had placed two glasses of iced tea on the breakfast bar. He sat on one of the stools. "Tonight looked like a success. Did you feel it was?"

Again they were talking about *her*, and she wanted to know more about *him*. "My cut was enough to pay my mortgage this month, so I'm grateful."

He turned his glass around on the counter. "You worked hard tonight. You had lots of individual consultations. Is that the way it always works?"

"Pretty much. How did you like the wine?"

"It was excellent. I tasted a dry white, a dry red and a sangria."

"A glass of each?"

He shook his head. "No. I would have needed a designated driver if I had done that. Just a taste of each. I concentrated on the hors d'oeuvres."

When she laughed, their gazes met. She was seated beside him and their arms brushed. The hairs on his forearm tickled her skin. However, remembering how he'd rebuffed her, she didn't want to be distracted at this moment. "Did you get leads of possible clients from Carlo?"

"Possibly. You never know how cold calls will turn out."

"He said you were interested in the Fortunes."

"Among others," Nash said with a nod. "There are many upstanding families in Austin."

Although he was answering her questions, she had the feeling there was something he wasn't telling her. Maybe he sensed she was going to ask more questions because he slid off his stool and picked up his glass. "I'll just take this up to my room if you don't mind."

"I don't mind."

As if he were reluctant to leave, he said, "You look pretty tonight."

For these events, she dressed up more than usual. Tonight she'd worn a black pantsuit with an expensive label, though she'd found it at the thrift store.

"Thank you," she said.

She slid off her stool, too, and suddenly they were standing very close.

"Did *you* have any wine tonight?" he asked.

She shook her head. "I like to remain clearheaded, especially when I'm painting." The truth was she didn't drink, not after seeing what alcohol had done to her mother. Though sometime maybe she should taste the Mendoza wines, just for the experience.

"And even when you're not," Nash guessed.

"And even when I'm not," she confirmed.

He reached out and touched her cheek, and it seemed as if he wanted to say something but then thought better of it. Instead he moved away from her toward the stairs. "See you tomorrow."

"See you tomorrow," she murmured. She had a feeling Nash Tremont was holding secrets of his own, but she couldn't fault him for that, because she held secrets, too.

Chapter Four

When Nash sat at a computer in the library the following day, he took his list from his pocket. Now he had more specific names to look up. An investigator never knew where a line of information could lead. So Nash was going to read everything he could get his hands or eyes on.

Carlo had been upfront with him about who had attended the Valentine's Day party. People with cell phones had taken lots of photos and posted them to their social media pages. Therefore, Carlo considered the information public knowledge. Nash had explained he was a financial consultant staying at the Bluebonnet Bed-and-Breakfast, and because Carlo respected Cassie, he'd considered her a recommendation for Nash.

Nash didn't like the subterfuge but sometimes it was necessary. Sometimes he had to consider the greater good, which in this case meant nailing a thief. In his estimation, Charlotte Robinson, Gerald's wife, was definitely that. One thing he knew for sure was that she was deceptive.

After his mom had gotten pregnant with him, she'd tried to contact Gerald. But Charlotte had intercepted her messages. In fact, she'd intimidated Nash's mother by threatening her. She'd warned his mom to stay away from her husband or there would be consequences. For that threat alone, Nash wanted to nail her. He didn't know how his mother maintained her sweetness rather than bitterness, but somehow through all the years she had. He respected her for that.

The first name on his list was Ben Fortune and his wife, Ella. Searching specifically for them, he found photographs of the couple at charity events along with Ben's twin brother, Wes, and his wife, Vivian. Although she wasn't on his list, that had led him to Lucie Fortune Chesterfield Parker, a member of the Fortune family who was almost British royalty. He discovered quickly that Chase Parker, her husband, was part of an oil family but had chosen his own path and now owned a horse rescue farm.

Apparently, Lucie was heavily involved in work with the Fortune Foundation, helping younger kids right here in Austin. The articles about Chase and Lucie led him to her sister Amelia, her husband, Quinn, and their daughter, Clementine Rose. He also found references to Charles, their brother. He soon realized there was nothing underhanded about the English side of the Fortune family. He could delve further but on first glance, they seemed to be upright citizens.

Another name on Nash's list was Keaton Whitfield, who was Ben's half sibling. He was a renowned architect.

It wasn't long before Nash realized many of the Fortunes had seemed to find true love. His biological father certainly hadn't, though his mother still believed she had been in love with him and he with her. Love could delude a person. It could make a person blind. He should know. He'd been blind to Sara's doubts about being in a relationship with a cop. Looking back, he wondered how he had *not* seen the signs. Or maybe she simply hadn't been honest with herself. Maybe she hadn't wanted to rock the boat of a convenient relationship.

Research consumed Nash for the morning. He quit around lunchtime and headed back to the B&B.

When he arrived, he thought he heard Cassie out on the sunporch, so he headed that way. She looked a bit harried as she fussed with a tripod and her phone. He watched as she stood in front of it and checked her phone and frowned. She made the tripod higher and did it again. Still adjusting it, she checked her phone and shook her head.

She'd been so preoccupied with what she was doing that she hadn't heard him come in or seen him standing there. Leaning against the doorjamb, he crossed one booted foot over the other. "Having a problem?" he asked.

As she glanced up at him, her cheeks pinkened a bit. For some reason, she was dressed in a cute dress that had a red-and-white pattern and a full swingy skirt. He appreciated the shorter style. He knew he should turn around and walk away, not get involved in what she was doing. But she seemed to be having a hard time of it, and he found he couldn't just walk away.

"I'm trying to set up my phone to take a video," she explained.

His curiosity got the best of him. "Why do you need a video?"

Standing up straight to face him, she pushed her hair back over her brow. Drawn to her more than he ever wanted to be, he followed the motion of her hand, noticing the wave that swept along her cheek. He felt a lot hotter than he had when he'd come in.

With a sigh, she sat in the chair near the easel. "My dream is to someday hire someone to run the B&B. What I really want to do is teach. My goal is to be hired as an art teacher in a school district." She was quiet for a moment and he waited. Finally, she explained, "I went for two interviews in the past few weeks, and the principals of those schools told me they don't have positions now but they'll keep my résumé on file."

Stepping closer to her, he noted, "That still doesn't explain the video."

"Both principals hinted that getting hired these days requires *more* than a résumé. Many applicants turn in a DVD of themselves teaching a lesson. That way, the principal gets a taste of an applicant's teaching method and expertise. I want to try making a DVD, but I have to practice."

"So do you want to record a lesson to a general audience? Or do you want to film a lesson with one of your students?"

Her eyes widened at the thought.

"You'd have to have their permission, of course, and their parents' permission, but it seems to me that would be more riveting."

"*If* an art lesson could be riveting," she said dryly. "That's what you were thinking, weren't you?"

"You think you know what I'm thinking?" he teased. If she did, she'd be running for the hills.

Her cheeks grew rosier. "Not that I know what you're thinking exactly, but most people would be thinking that. Sometimes art is very internal. It's up to the teacher to bring out what's going on inside onto the paper or canvas. That isn't always easy to do. A lesson with a child could fail miserably."

"If it does, you just dump the video," he suggested.

"I don't know, Nash. It would be a lot safer just to teach to a general audience."

Now he frowned. "You don't seem like a woman who doesn't want to take risks. No risk, no gain. Isn't that the saying?"

"I thought the saying was no pain, no gain."

He laughed. "Those two are very different. But really, Cassie, the excitement of a child learning how to do something new could be riveting on a DVD. And it would be so much easier if you had somebody recording the video rather than you trying to set it up. I'd be happy to record for you, if you did it within the next couple of weeks. I can even put it on a DVD for you on my laptop."

She was already shaking her head. "I couldn't take advantage of you like that."

Leaving his relaxed stance behind, he walked over to her and stood right in front of her. "From what I've seen, and from what Mrs. Garcia told me, you're always doing things for others. I've got to wonder if anyone does things for you."

"I…uh…don't know what to say to that. Sure, people do things for me."

"Like?" he asked.

She thought for a few seconds. "At the grocery store the checkout boy often carries bags to my car for me when I have too many."

Nash gave her a look that obviously made her search her mind for something else. "Renata—Mrs. Garcia—often gives me embroidered handkerchiefs she finds in her drawers. She wants to pass them down and they're lovely. And the kids—the kids all give me smiles and joy."

"How about your friends?" Nash asked.

"I'm too busy to socialize much."

The investigator in Nash saw the red flag. Usually when someone didn't have friends, that meant they didn't want to get close to anybody. Either they didn't have self-confidence or self-worth...or they were hiding something. He had no idea what Cassie would possibly be hiding.

His reaction to Cassie always disconcerted him. He was so attracted to her he should hightail it away from Austin...or at least away from the B&B. However, instead of leaving, he reached out and touched her cheek. "You deserve to have nice things done for you. You wouldn't be taking advantage of me. I'd enjoy doing it. It would be a break from business."

Cassie seemed to think about it. She was staring at him with those beautiful chocolate eyes. All he had to do was slide his hand up her neck into her hair and bring her close. But he didn't do that. He took a step away.

She seemed to recognize that step for what it was. He was removing himself from temptation. She looked flustered, but she quickly recovered. "All right. I'll let you video me before you leave. But that means extra cinnamon rolls for you."

He laughed. "You've got a deal. Did you eat lunch yet?"

"No. I've been occupied trying to do this," she said with a frown.

"Do you have guests to take care of?"

"Only you," she joked. "The Warners are out for the day."

"Since you look so pretty all dressed up, how would you like to go out to lunch?"

His offer took her by surprise. "Oh, I don't know."

Although he knew he shouldn't—for so many reasons—he pushed. "I passed an outside café on my way back here. It looked nice. We could sit outside and enjoy the pretty day. I mean, really, how long has it been since you were out to lunch?"

"It has been a while. I usually just grab something in between errands or B&B business or art lessons."

"Then let's go. You can tell me again why you'd like to be a teacher rather than an artist."

A short time later, as Cassie and Nash walked down the street, she was totally aware of him. He was wearing his boots, jeans, a tan polo shirt, and of course, the black Stetson. Even in the polo shirt, she could see the muscles in his arms. Maybe financial consultants worked out. That would explain it. She didn't know what else would. Good genes?

Sometimes, the way he questioned her, he reminded her of a lawyer. But she supposed financial consultants had to ask questions, too. They had to get to know their clients, their needs and wants, their intentions for the future. So he was practiced at asking questions, she supposed. They must also practice not talking about themselves.

Now she looked over at him. "What did you really think about the Paint and Sip party?"

"What do you mean—what did I really think?"

"Does it serve a purpose, fill a need, or is it just a money-making scheme?"

He took a few seconds to think about it. But then he decided, "Everyone needs a job, Cassie, and they need to pay the bills. Using your talent to do that isn't a bad thing."

She'd never really had a moral compass in her parents, certainly not in her mother. She supposed she'd always looked toward her church and her priest for answers, and she found most of them there.

She could feel Nash studying her as they walked, the spring breeze blowing her dress against her legs.

"I'll tell you what I think of it," he said.

She braced herself for the worst.

"I think everyone needs a creative outlet. It could be writing in a journal. It could be building sandcastles. For you, it's painting. At the Paint and Sip, you shared that gift with everyone else. Do I think it's a little manufactured? Maybe. After all, don't some of your paintings take a week to do, not just one night?"

"Make that weeks, sometimes."

"Exactly. But what you're doing is teaching a technique. Beginners like immediate gratification. That's what you're giving them. And if they sip wine and enjoy themselves along the way, what's wrong with that?"

"I suppose nothing. But if I get a teaching position, I think that's one of the first things I'd drop. I'd want to keep volunteering at the art center and maybe give private lessons."

"You want to teach children to be true artists rather than teaching kids the techniques just to finish a painting."

"Yes. I want to teach them about techniques and the Masters, and the great museums."

"And I imagine you'll be a terrific teacher."

She didn't have to comment because they'd reached the outdoor café. Green-and-white-striped awnings covered the outside seating area. They migrated to a table that was near a wall and Nash pulled a chair out for her. She'd never had anybody do that before. As she sat and he pushed her in, she glanced over her shoulder. His face was very close to hers. In fact, her cheek brushed the rim of his hat.

"I'll get rid of this," he said, and went to hang his Stetson on one of the hat pegs tacked on the outside wall. She watched him as he ran his hand through his hair a few times.

After he sat across from her, he smiled. "The reason cowboys never take off their hats is that their hair's a mess underneath."

She broke into a genuine laugh. "So you're not a real cowboy?"

"I'm not even half a cowboy. I just enjoy boots, jeans and a good Stetson. You know, men wear them even in Oklahoma. In fact, as I was growing up, I thought ball caps and Stetsons were the only two kinds of hats there were for men."

"Are you serious or are you pulling my leg?"

"I'm very serious. Ever been to Oklahoma?"

She shook her head. "I've never been out of Texas."

He cocked his head and studied her again.

Breaking eye contact, she watched the passersby. Nash did, too. Their waiter came to take their order. Nash chose the roast beef panini with caramelized onions while she chose the turkey club sandwich.

"Order whatever you want," Nash said. "I'm paying."

"No, you're not," she protested. "We're going Dutch or we don't get lunch."

They stared at each other for a few seconds until the waiter looked at Cassie. "Would you like to order something else?"

"No, just the club and a glass of lemonade."

"Coming up shortly," the waiter said and went inside.

"You can be a tough cookie when you want to be," Nash admitted with some surprise.

"Not used to women who stand up for themselves?" she asked with a grin.

"Oh, you wound me! Of course I like women who stand up for themselves. I wouldn't want to be in a relationship with any other kind. Guessing what the other person is thinking doesn't make for good communication."

"You've had that problem?"

"Could be," Nash answered enigmatically.

He'd done it again. He'd shut down a perfectly good conversation. Silence dropped between them for a few minutes until Cassie bumped Nash's elbow. "See that man walking along the street?"

Nash looked the way Cassie's chin was pointed. She thought she saw a flicker of something in Nash's eyes but it was gone faster than she'd imagined it.

"Are you just showing me a representative Texas cowboy?" he asked.

"No." She kept her voice low. "That's Nate Fortune."

Nate definitely was eye candy for anybody looking his way. He was over six feet tall, with dark brown hair and brown eyes.

She noticed Nash studying Nate Fortune. His next words sounded as if he'd chosen them carefully. "I think the Fortune family has made every newspaper in big cities and every blog on the internet. Do you ever wonder what it would be like to be connected to a family like the Fortunes? Do they really have brotherly and sisterly relationships? Or is everything they do cutthroat, for business's sake?"

"They're a dynasty in themselves," Cassie responded. "I should hope among all those relatives there would be some strong connections. I would have loved to have a brother or sister. How about you? Do you have siblings?"

He hesitated a moment, then shook his head. "No, I don't."

"Were you lonely as a boy?"

Nash shrugged. She thought he was going to shut down this conversation, too. Instead, his gaze met hers and he answered her. "Some of the time I was lonely, but most of the time I was too busy to be lonely. I got jobs wherever I could find them to help my mom make ends meet."

Cassie wanted to tell him that she'd done that, too, but she didn't want to get into that subject, because he thought her parents were dead. If she never really told him her story, would she ever really get to know his?

A few hours later, Nash wasn't sure why he was calling his friend in Oklahoma. Maybe Cassie pointing out

Nate Fortune had unsettled him. He had to watch not only his words but his actions around her. Because of his research at the library, he'd recognized Nate Fortune. Nate had been one of the family pictured at the Valentine's Day party at the Mendoza Winery. Nash had an almost photographic memory, especially when it came to faces. That helped in his investigations.

He scrolled through his contacts and called Dave. He hoped his former partner was off shift. He and Dave Preston had gone to the Police Academy together and risen up through the ranks. When Cassie had asked him if he'd ever wanted a brother, he'd thought of Dave. His friend was the closest thing to a brother he'd ever get.

"Is this good news or bad news?" Dave asked when he answered.

"Maybe it's no news," Nash replied. "Maybe I just wanted to hear your voice. You know, a taste of home and all that."

"You haven't called Oklahoma home for a while now, even though your mom wants you to."

Nash sighed. "I know that. How's she doing? She's always cheery when I call her but I don't know if that's the truth."

"She misses you."

"She also misses the future I was planning on having, the one that would give her grandkids."

"You sound as if it's never going to happen."

Nash immediately thought of Cassie. But he answered his friend with, "Probably not."

Changing the subject, Dave asked, "So what have you found in your research?" Dave was the only one besides Nash's mother who knew what he was about here in Austin.

"Nothing yet that has led anywhere, but I'm still curious how these people live."

"'These people?' You mean your relatives?"

"They're *not* my relatives, Dave."

"You know what they say—blood is thicker than water."

Nash retorted, "And I say if you haven't known them as family all your life, they're not family."

Dave continued to disagree. "Open your mind a little, Nash. You might like one or two of them."

Nash thought about Chase Parker, who owned the horse rescue ranch, and his wife, Lucie, who was a Fortune. He remembered what he'd found about her helping kids. Was that all just PR? He also remembered her sister Amelia's husband was a rancher. But those were two of the female Fortunes. As far as the men went, he just didn't know.

"One thing I've learned, or I guess I've verified, is that Gerald Robinson was unethical, indiscriminate and generally someone I don't want to know."

"What if you came face-to-face with him?" Dave asked.

"It's not going to happen. That's not why I'm here."

"Are you planning on staying in Austin longer than a month?" Dave asked.

"Not unless I want to quit my job."

"With your résumé, I'm sure you could get a job in Austin if you wanted it. Think how much easier it would be to investigate the Fortunes."

"Okay, now you're mocking me. I'm going to end this call."

"I'm serious about the job, Nash. If you feel you have to be there, maybe a move wouldn't be a bad thing."

Nash thought about Cassie again. Her life was here. "I'm just taking it day by day. One leads to the next."

"And what's next?" Dave inquired.

"A drive around some of the Fortune addresses. I want to see how they live."

"How's that going to help you?"

"Call it curiosity. Maybe my eyes need a break from the computer. Besides, you know how stakeouts go. You never know what will turn up."

"No, you never know," Dave agreed. "Be careful, Nash. Nobody knows you're there but me and your mom."

"And the two of you need to stop worrying. The owner of the bed-and-breakfast would send out an alarm if I don't come back."

"She had a pretty voice."

Before Nash could stop himself, he said, "She *is* pretty."

Dave's silence met that remark, and Nash didn't intend to elaborate on it.

"I meant it when I said to be careful, Nash, and I'm not only talking about physically. You could end up in the middle of family you don't want to meet. They might not like another relative turning up. And as far as the pretty voice and the pretty face of the owner of the Bluebonnet Bed-and-Breakfast…"

"I've got to go, Dave. I'll check in again next week."

"I'm counting on it."

When Nash ended the call, he had to smile. Dave could be irritating at times, but Nash wouldn't want to go through life without him. His friend was right about one thing, though—he *did* need to be careful…with both the Fortunes and with Cassie.

Chapter Five

It was 5 a.m. on Sunday when Nash awakened, not exactly sure why. Then he realized that he'd heard the pipes creaking. It was coming from the downstairs bathroom.

He guessed Cassie was taking a shower. No, he was not going to think about *that* too long. Punching his pillow and closing his eyes again, he wondered why she was getting up so early. She didn't serve breakfast until 8 a.m. He considered the idea that maybe she just wanted to get up and paint. Then why take a shower?

After another half hour of tossing and turning, he figured he might as well just get dressed and go downstairs and find out what Cassie was up to. Once on the first floor, his nose twitched. He smelled dough of some kind. Checking the kitchen, he didn't find Cassie but rather two huge ceramic bowls covered by towels.

He peeked under one of them. Yeast bread. It would probably take some time for it to rise.

Instinct made him go to the front door and look out. He spotted Cassie walking about half a block down the street. Not knowing what he intended to do, he decided to follow her. Maybe the investigator in him just needed something to investigate other than old photographs and news stories.

He hadn't tailed anyone for a long time, and he didn't know if he should be doing it now. But he was curious.

He didn't have to be curious for long. He was thirty yards behind Cassie when he saw her stop and then go up the steps of a church. Did he really want to follow her there? It would certainly bring back memories.

Once he reached the steps himself, he climbed them, then opened one of the wooden doors that led into the Church of the Good Shepherd.

In the narthex the doors were propped open, leading into the nave of the church. Straight ahead, hanging behind the altar, was a lifelike statue of the Good Shepherd. On the left in the rainbow light of a stained glass window was a statue of Mary and a rack of candles beneath her. In the sparsely populated church, he caught sight of Cassie about three rows back from the altar. Nash found himself slipping into one of the back pews, blessing himself, remembering his childhood.

The Mass was a ritual he hadn't been part of in a long time, but he found he still knew when to stand and sit and when to kneel. The homily was short, probably because this was such an early Mass and the priest knew everyone had somewhere to go.

At the end of the Mass, Nash wasn't sure whether to slip out so Cassie didn't know he'd ever been there, or to stay put and wait until she left. If she noticed him, well, then she noticed him.

It didn't take long for the church to empty. Nash spotted Cassie still sitting in her pew. He decided not to be secretive about this, at least. Walking up the side aisle, he slid into the pew with her.

She glanced at him and her eyes widened in surprise. She asked, "Were you here for Mass?"

"I was." He didn't feel a need to give an explanation.

"You're Catholic?"

"Lapsed," he said with a shrug. "My mother took me to church during my childhood, and I went to Catholic school until eighth grade. Then I went to a public high school."

If he was any reader of thoughts, he saw a myriad of expressions flit over Cassie's face. The main one—surprise he was telling her this.

"Why did you stop going?" she asked.

"You know how teenagers are," he said. "They question everything."

"I questioned," she empathized. "But—" She hesitated for a moment. "But when things in my life were tough, I gravitated back toward my faith."

"My mother wished I had done that."

"Why didn't you?"

He didn't see any harm in telling her. He wouldn't be revealing anything. "I had a father who let's just say wasn't the best guy. He left my mother high and dry. I never knew him. That didn't seem to bother me so much when I was a kid but when I was a teenager, when friends were going on fishing trips with their dads or camping or working on school projects together, anger set in. That anger just seemed to be at odds with faith."

"And now?"

"I guess I just got out of the habit of believing. Life and my job, especially, just seemed to take all my attention."

After they sat there awhile longer in silence, Cassie said, "I really have to get back or the bread dough I prepared will proof too much. But I'd like to light a candle first. You don't have to stay."

"I'll wait," he said, actually looking forward to walking her back to the bed-and-breakfast.

Cassie had worn a peasant blouse with three-quarter sleeves and a skirt that flowed to her calves. Her flats were soundless on the tile floor as she slipped by him out of the pew and walked up to light a candle. After kneeling at the statue for a minute or so—long enough to say a prayer, Nash guessed—she stood and walked back to the pew.

He rose to his feet and met her at the aisle. Together they walked out. The blues, yellows and reds from the stained glass windows flickered across Cassie's face as they walked down the aisle. Her hair swung against her neck and Nash was struck again by her vulnerability. Did she seem more vulnerable this morning because they were in church?

Cassie took a church bulletin from a stand by the door. Then he opened the outside door for her and they stepped into the sunlight and a beautiful Sunday morning in Austin.

They walked down the steps together, their arms brushing. That touch of skin on skin felt right, and Nash kept his thoughts from going further than that.

On the sidewalk once more, heading toward the bed-and-breakfast, Nash couldn't stop the question that echoed in his mind. She'd asked him some personal questions; now it was his turn. "Did you light a candle for your parents?"

Cassie seemed to take a deep breath before she answered. He guessed she still missed them. Instead of answering him, she simply nodded.

He remained silent as they passed a mixture of apartment houses and single-family dwellings, some in brick, some in stucco, some in stone.

"Do you have a busy day planned?" he finally asked her.

"I do. After making breakfast—we're having quiche and homemade bread if you're interested—I'm going to bake cookies and fruit breads to freeze. That way if I'm too busy during the week, I can pull them out. I'm also going to have guests checking in today. So there are rooms to get ready and freshen up as well as towels to put out. The Warners are leaving so I'll be cleaning their room. It will be a busy day."

"Do you have help?"

"Help? Such as a maid?" Cassie laughed. "There isn't any money in the budget to hire a maid. I'm it. Do you have a busy day planned?"

"Actually, I do," he said. "I'll be out most of the day." He didn't tell her he had a list of addresses where Fortunes lived. He was going to scope out their living arrangements and maybe get a glimpse of their lives.

When they reached the B&B, Cassie waved to Mrs. Garcia, who was out on her front porch. She was wearing a flowered dress and carrying her purse. Nash accompanied Cassie as they walked over to the widow's porch.

"Good morning," Mrs. Garcia said. "Were you two out for a stroll?"

"We were at church," Cassie said.

"That's where I'm headed now."

The day was already warming up and Nash remembered what Mrs. Garcia had said about her arthritis. "Why don't I drive you," he said to Mrs. Garcia.

"But aren't you going to eat breakfast?" the older woman asked.

"It won't be ready for about half an hour," Cassie said. "Maybe a little longer. I have to put the bread in to bake."

"If you make them into rolls, they won't take as long to bake," Mrs. Garcia said.

"That's a great idea," Cassie agreed. "And when you get home, I'll bring a couple over to you."

Mrs. Garcia beamed. "That would be lovely. And, young man, I think I'll take you up on your offer."

Nash went up Mrs. Garcia's steps and offered her his arm. This wasn't exactly the way he'd intended to spend his Sunday morning, but right now, it seemed like the best way to start the day.

After he drove Mrs. Garcia to church, he had breakfast with Cassie and the Warners. The couple was checking out after breakfast and he knew Cassie had a busy day, so he didn't linger.

What he did do caused feelings to roil inside of him. He drove past where several of the Fortunes lived. That took well into the afternoon. But then he went where he probably shouldn't have. He parked down the street from Gerald Robinson's estate. It had a stone wall surrounding it and an iron gate. According to what Nash had found about it online, the house looked like a Mediterranean castle. It was easy to see the Robinsons had an elevated lifestyle. So elevated that Charlotte never wanted to lose it. That had been one of the reasons she'd kept his mother from getting in touch with Gerald, or Jerome, or whatever anybody wanted to call him. The whole name change idea irked Nash. Supposedly Jerome wanted to change his name to build a life on his own. Really? He couldn't even keep his first name? None of it made sense to Nash.

During Nash's stakeout, no one came and went at the Robinson house. Nash felt the bitterness he had always pushed away rise up in his throat. He knew anger and bitterness weren't good for him, and he realized that maybe he was following this money trail of Charlotte's for revenge's sake. If he took her down, he took Gerald down.

Did he want to do that to his biological father? He'd told himself over and over again Gerald Robinson had been no more than a sperm donor. Yet his mother considered the man much more. She said she understood why he'd stayed with Charlotte. But did she really?

What if bringing Gerald and Charlotte down put a wedge between Nash and his mom? Would all of this have been worth it?

Cassie handed the Stengles their keys. They were an adorable couple on their honeymoon. They were from Kansas but they were taking a road trip to San Antonio, wandering here and there along the way. They were about her age, and she was happy to see two people who had found each other.

Cassie told them, "If you need anything, just call the front desk. My cell phone is also on the information sheet, so if you can't reach me at the desk, then call my cell. Will you be staying in for supper tonight?"

"Oh, no," they both said at the same time. "We're going out on the town," Tom Stengle told her. "We want to see everything we can see."

"You'll find a list of restaurants and attractions in your room near your phone."

Tom said, "I'll carry our bags upstairs." Cassie offered to help but he brushed her help away.

As Tom went up the stairs, his wife Annabelle leaned close to her. "We're going to spend some time in our room until dinner tonight. I hope there's a Do Not Disturb sign."

Cassie gave the newlywed a nod. "There certainly is."

Cassie had noticed Nash had come in while she was checking in the Stengles. He looked tired. Something about his expression bothered her. The lines around his eyes cut in deep. Maybe *troubled* was a better word than *tired*. He'd gone into the guest lounging area and drawn a cup of coffee. He was just sitting there on the couch now, broodingly staring into his mug.

She thought about their conversation at the church that morning and about his kindness to Renata. She didn't like to see anybody going through troubles.

The bed-and-breakfast was quiet now. The Stengles were in their room and she had a feeling they'd be there awhile. The other couple who had checked in had gone right out again. Cassie had finished everything she'd intended to do today. The way it looked, she might not even have to cook supper except for herself.

Crossing to the sitting area, she sank down on the couch beside Nash. "Rough day?" she asked.

He took a gulp of his coffee. "Rough enough."

"Anything you want to talk about? I hear talking relieves stress." She kept her voice light, hoping to get a feel for what was going on with him.

He just shook his head.

She realized she was prying and she had no right to do that. "As a financial adviser, I guess you have to be discreet. I shouldn't be asking any questions. I'm sorry."

But as she started to rise to her feet, Nash caught her hand. She felt his touch throughout her whole body. When she looked into his eyes, she didn't know what she saw. It looked remarkably like guilt. Why would Nash feel guilty?

"I'm going to trust my gut on this," he mumbled.

"Trust your gut?" She didn't understand at all.

"Can we go someplace more private?"

If any other man had asked her that, she'd refuse. But it was easy for her to see Nash's request had nothing to do with a line or romance.

She had a dilemma. She could offer to go out on the screened-in porch with him. That would be private. But even more private would be the sitting area in her room. She'd never asked a man into her room before.

"How are you at lighting fires?" she asked.

He looked perplexed.

"It's cool tonight and I have a fireplace in the sitting area in my suite. I never seem to stack everything right to get it started. We could light a fire and talk there. I might even be able to rustle up a cinnamon roll or two."

He studied her face for what seemed to be a very long time. Then he nodded. "I'm good at lighting fires."

She walked him down the hall into her suite, which was really just one big room with an en suite bath. But she had it divided into a small sitting area with a love seat and rocking chair at the fireplace, and a bedroom area with its single bed, nightstand and small dresser.

She pointed to the fireplace, where, on the hearth, kindling and a few logs lay in a basket.

He gave her a half smile. "You're making this easy."

"Matches are on the mantel," she told him as she left the room.

In the kitchen, as she took the cinnamon rolls from the tinfoil packet, she realized her hands were shaking. That was silly. Nash was just going to unburden himself. She shouldn't think anything of it, not anything at all. But as she carried the rolls and another cup of coffee for herself back to the sitting room, she knew she was going to get in deeper with Nash and wasn't sure about that at all.

Nash had a glow coming from the fireplace and he was sitting on the love seat with his mug of coffee. She settled next to him, setting the rolls on the small coffee table.

As he looked around her bedroom, he asked, "Is everything in your life in 3-D and color?"

She laughed. She liked bright colors and used them everywhere. There was a bright blue bedspread crisscrossed with violet and lime on her bed and matching curtains. They stood out against her lemon-yellow walls. A mobile with abstract colorful shapes hung above a file cabinet where she kept folders for each of her art students.

"Do you have something against color?" she joked.

"Not at all," he said with a shake of his head. "I'm just not sure how you sleep in here." Her love seat was also a shade of violet, and the armchair was lime green.

Cassie sat a little sideways and looked at him. "You don't really want to talk about the color of my room, do you?"

His brow furrowed. His eyes looked pained as he frowned. "No. I want to come clean with you."

Come clean? About what? She felt frightened for a few seconds, maybe even panicked. Then she remembered there was nothing to fear. She kept silent.

"I'm not in town as a financial consultant," he revealed, watching her carefully.

She must have made a little gasp.

He quickly went on, "I'm a cop on independent assignment."

A cop. Now she felt a bit of panic all over again. She remembered cops taking her mother away. She'd never forget it. "What does that mean?" she asked, totally taken aback. She didn't know how she felt about Nash being a member of law enforcement. After all, her mother was in prison...and he didn't know.

Nash set his mug on the coffee table. "I'm following up on a case that my boss didn't want me to pursue. I took vacation time to do it."

"Is the work dangerous?" she asked.

"No, it's not dangerous. It's mostly research. I'm not carrying a weapon if that's what you're worried about." When he turned to face her more directly, their knees were touching. "I'm supposed to be incognito. I guess you could say undercover. But I'm sorry I didn't tell you the truth up front."

The truth. Her life wasn't completely honest and she hated that. "You didn't know me. Why should you trust me? Besides, you didn't have to tell me now, either. You're entitled to your secrets. Everybody is."

"I suppose," he said begrudgingly.

Their knees were still touching and neither of them had moved away. The fabric of his jeans rubbed a bit against the cotton of her skirt.

"Why did you tell me now?" she asked softly.

"I'm not exactly sure," he admitted. "I don't trust people easily. That's an occupational hazard. But I do believe *you* can be trusted."

Cassie felt honored that he thought so. But she also felt guilty because she was keeping secrets from him. However, especially now that she knew he was a cop, she couldn't tell him about her mother.

"I don't trust easily, either," she confessed, but she didn't volunteer why.

Cassie was still trying to absorb everything Nash had said as they stared into the fire. Moments later, she turned to glance at his face. His jaw was set and his mouth was a thin line. She suspected there was a lot more to his story than what he'd told her.

"Is that all you want to tell me?" she asked.

"I should just shut up," he muttered.

"Why? I'm certainly not going to tell anybody anything. If you need to get it off your chest, feel free."

"Off my chest isn't off my mind. I'm personally involved in this."

"In the investigation?"

"Yes. And I'm sure that's part of the reason my boss wants me to drop it. We've had resolution in the main part of the case, but I stumbled on this other thread."

"What you're saying is hard for me to understand because I don't know the basics."

"The basics are—the suspect that I'm investigating is quite possibly my biological father's wife."

So many questions ran through Cassie's head, she didn't know what to ask first. "Do you *know* your biological father?"

"You mean 'know' like he lived around me or I lived around him?"

"Yes. Have you spent time with him?"

"Never." Nash's voice was firm and there was more in his tone that she was sure he didn't want her to hear.

"He left?" she asked.

"Oh, yes. He definitely left. He was married, but my mother loved him anyway. She thinks more highly of him than I do."

"Did you know him at all?"

"We've never had any contact, and that's a good way to keep it, especially now."

"He's in Austin?"

"Yes, he and his wife."

"You know, don't you, if you do get the goods on your biological father's wife, you might be ruining any chance you have of getting to know your dad."

Nash went rigid and snapped, "He's not my father." There was so much bitterness in Nash's voice that Cassie recoiled.

Nash saw it. "Cassie, I'm sorry. I don't talk about this. I never talk about it. And this is why. This man is not a good man. He's had other affairs. My mother tried to contact him about me, but his wife intercepted her. She threatened her and my mother isn't the type to push."

Cassie realized this was only the tip of the iceberg. The fact that he was both professionally and personally involved in this case had to be tearing him apart.

When Nash reached a hand out to her, she took his.

He shook his head. "I'm sorry I involved you."

"I'm not sorry." She wasn't. Something about Nash touched her deeply.

Reaching out, he stroked her cheek and then he pushed her hair behind her ear. "You are so sweet," he murmured, and then he leaned in.

Cassie didn't move away. Moments later his lips were on hers, creating a fire much more dangerous than the one that was snapping at logs in the fireplace. She knew this kiss could get her in big trouble, but she still responded to it, responded to him. Her fingers tightened on his shoulders and Nash brought her closer.

Suddenly, however, reality seemed to hit them both. As Cassie tore away, Nash leaned back, too, and rubbed his hand down over his face.

Then he gazed at her with questions in his eyes. "What was that?" he asked.

"I'm not sure," she answered.

Nash rose to his feet. "I'd better go, for both our sakes. Agreed?"

"Agreed," she said with determination, knowing that was best for both of them. But as Nash left her room and the fire still burned, she knew they weren't done with each other yet.

Chapter Six

That night after dinner out, Nash went to his room. But he was restless. He didn't feel like staring at his laptop screen, either to work or to stream a movie. He couldn't forget about that kiss with Cassie. It had practically melted his boots.

He decided to search her out because maybe they should talk about it. He'd seen a lot of denial in his line of work, and it didn't solve anything. Sure, he could deny the kiss and Cassie could deny the kiss and they could walk around like it had never happened. But whenever they looked at each other, whenever they were around each other, it would be there.

First he went downstairs to find her. But she wasn't in the kitchen or the guest area, or out on the porch. Should he go back to the scene of the crime, so to speak?

But the door to her suite was closed and when he rapped, she didn't answer.

He called softly, "Cassie?"

Either she wasn't inside or she was ignoring him. Still, from what he knew about her so far, he didn't think she'd do that. There was one other place she could be. After he jogged up the stairs, he took time to notice what he'd been in too much of a hurry to see before. Down at the end of the hall the attic stairs were pulled down. She'd probably escaped for a while to paint. Should he bother her?

At least they'd have privacy up there to talk without him entering her suite. That might be good.

The stairs creaked as he climbed them, so she heard him coming. She had a white craft light positioned over her painting. When she looked over her shoulder and saw him, she didn't smile. Was she remembering their kiss?

Once again, he glanced around the room at all of the paintings. The landscapes were different from anybody else's he'd ever seen. They were bright and cheerful and would warm up any room. There were a few abstracts and he had to smile at the riot of colors. They reminded him of her house.

After she finished a stroke on the canvas, she dipped her brush into a jar and left it there. Before he asked about the kiss, he approached with a mundane question. "Relaxing?"

She rolled her shoulders and stretched her neck. "I'm trying to."

He didn't know if there was an underlying message in that response, but he reacted as if there was. "I suppose my being up here isn't helping that."

She turned on her stool to face him. She was wearing a bright blue Oxford shirt that came to her knees. The long sleeves were rolled up. He knew it was supposed to be a smock to protect her clothes from the paint, but she looked damn sexy.

Instead of getting to the subject he came up to discuss, he looked around at the paintings again. "Have you shown your work in any galleries?"

She stood and came over to him. "Not lately. I applied for the Art Alliance Showing at the Palmer Center this weekend, but I was turned down."

That astonished him. "Turned down? That doesn't seem possible."

He studied her face as she struggled to explain and be fair at the same time. "Artists from all over the country enter their work. I'm not sure how they decide exactly. As with most artistic work, opinions are subjective."

He waved his arm over the attic. "Do you have photos of all these?"

"Some of them."

"You should take photos of all of them and put an extensive portfolio together."

After she hesitated a few moments, she revealed, "A few years ago I won a contest. After the fact, one of the judges bought three of my paintings at the exorbitant prices that my agent suggested. I sold two more to an art patron from the gallery where the paintings were displayed. Those sales were enough for a down payment on the B&B. I never would have been able to get started without that. But since I've run the B&B, I cut ties with my agent. I haven't had time to promote my work or even set up a website. It's always which thing on the to-do list takes priority, and this is never it because it's so hit-and-miss."

"You know that's the first time you've told me anything about your past." He couldn't help but wonder about it. He'd shared his and hoped she'd open up with him.

She didn't respond to his statement. Rather she asked, "Why did you come up here, Nash?"

As he expected, she was forthright. "I thought maybe we should talk about that kiss. It's going to be difficult to ignore. I'll be here another three weeks and I didn't want our interaction to be awkward."

Her eyes were studying him as if she were searching for the truth. "It doesn't have to be awkward between us. We just go on from here."

"And forget the sizzle we feel every time we're in the same room?" he questioned with a raised brow.

"We have to," she reminded him. "You're going back to Mississippi. What would be the point in…anything happening?"

Just as he thought. She didn't indulge in flings. Neither did he. Nevertheless, a fling right now seemed just the ticket to forget what he was doing. Just the ticket to distract himself from the Fortunes. And to bring pleasure to them both.

They were standing close enough that he caught Cassie's scent. It was flowery and drew him toward her. He leaned a little closer and so did she.

But then he shook his head. "If we don't want that kiss to happen again, I'd better go downstairs. You can go back to relaxing and painting."

She didn't protest or ask him to stay, so he knew she wanted him to go. After he crossed to the stairs, he glanced over his shoulder at her. She was still watching him. She turned away first and he continued down to the second floor.

Once in his room, he went straight for his laptop. Pulling out the chair, he settled in at the small desk. This time he wasn't searching for the Fortune name. He went to a website he often used and typed in *Cassandra Calloway*. If she'd won a contest he might be able to find out something about it.

He did. But not much. Just her name and the information that she'd won first place in the Texas Winter Fest's Art Contest. The article said she was from Bryan. At least he knew something more now than he did before. And maybe, in the days to come, she'd open up to him and share more than a kiss.

Cassie had really tried hard not to remember that the Art Alliance Showing was at the Palmer Center this weekend. She didn't know if she wanted to see why her work was turned down or if everybody else's was so much better. The two couples who were staying at the B&B along with Nash had already eaten their breakfast and left. Cassie had seen Nash's SUV parked along the street, so either he had gotten up early and walked somewhere, or he didn't care about breakfast. He hadn't slept in any of the days he'd been here. But who knew? Today could be different.

He hadn't been around much this week. He hadn't sought her out. Was he sorry he'd confided in her? Did he regret the bond that had formed because he'd shared a secret? She had to stop thinking about him.

An hour later, she was slicing and dicing vegetables

for the evening meal. One of the new couples who had checked in this week had said they'd be here tonight.

When she heard the stair steps creak, she was surprised to see Nash. He wasn't dressed for a business meeting today. He wore blue jeans and his old brown boots along with a black Henley shirt. The Stetson was missing, though, which meant he wasn't going out.

"Not working today?" she asked as he came into the kitchen.

"Not today. Even investigators need a day off now and then. I had an idea, though. How's your day looking?"

"No new arrivals today. Dinner for a couple tonight. I should do some chores, but..."

"But?" he asked, his head cocked.

"What was your idea?" She didn't know if it included her or not, but the way he'd said it, it might.

"I thought you might want to go to the arts festival."

She frowned. "I was going to skip it this year."

"Because you weren't accepted to show?"

Too perceptive. He was just too perceptive. "That doesn't sound very good, does it? I should want to see other artists' work, right?"

"From the ads, it looks like the arts festival has more to offer than paintings."

"All right. Since I don't have a good excuse not to go—"

He gave her an offended look.

She laughed. "I think it sounds like fun to go with you. Just give me a couple of minutes to stow away the veggies and get ready."

A half hour later, they'd parked and were walking toward the Palmer Center. Nash had been quiet in the car and she'd wondered what he was thinking about. She'd left him to his thoughts as she considered hers. Had he asked her along today because he'd kissed her and maybe wanted to do it again? Just how did she feel about that? If she thought about it, she felt weak-kneed. All week her mind had skittered around the idea of kissing him again. Not only kissing. She wanted to be held in those strong arms.

As they walked into the Palmer Center, Cassie felt she had to make conversation. She said, "Art City Austin started out from a local street fair and progressed to this. This year they welcomed over a hundred individual artists from across the country, and there are twenty galleries from across Texas who are showcasing works."

"This place is something else," Nash commented, looking around. "The stone and tile, all the glass, the covered balcony on the second floor. It's really amazing."

"It's one of our Austin landmarks."

They turned down a hall that was decorated with paintings on the wall. Cassie turned to Nash and asked, "Why did you really want to come here today?"

He studied her for a few seconds as if he was gauging his reply. But then he said, "I'm tired of researching and going through public documents. There are so many and most of them don't have anything to do with my biological father's wife." He grimaced. Then he said, "It seems odd to be talking about it with you."

"Why?"

"Because I've kept what I'm doing under wraps for so long. I could be looking at public documents at home, but here in Austin, where the couple lives, I thought I could find out more."

"Like putting all the puzzle pieces together," she suggested.

"Exactly. And what better way to get away from the puzzle for a time than to go to an arts festival with a pretty girl."

She wrinkled her nose at him. "You don't have to resort to flattery."

Pure surprise registered on his handsome face. "Resort? You think I'm handing you a line?"

With a resigned shrug, she admitted, "The truth is, Nash, I really haven't dated, not for a very long time. So I'm not sure I'd know a line when someone was handing it to me."

He took her by the shoulders and looked deep into her eyes. "That wasn't a line, Cassie. I don't do lines. You are pretty and sexy and talented. End of discussion."

She blinked, but then she asked, "Is that your cop voice you're using?"

He laughed. "It usually works. Is it working on you?"

"No. If someone tells me the discussion ended, that just makes me want to continue it."

He shook his head. "You're one of those, huh?"

She laughed again. Then seriously she said, "I suppose you've run into people of all personalities, both male and female."

"I have. When I was a beat cop in Oklahoma, the work was rough,. We put in long hours, preventing domestic violence if we could, preventing shootings or getting in the middle of those shootings. But in spite of all that, I actually enjoy talking to ordinary people—for instance, a kid who is usually afraid of cops. Once he talked to me, then he wasn't afraid. I like the time I spent in schools, giving workshops on safety for kids."

"So why did you leave it?"

"I needed a new life."

To Cassie that sounded as if Nash's heart had been broken, but he didn't seem willing to talk to her about that. They hadn't known each other well enough or long enough, and this wasn't exactly the place to have that kind of discussion.

Still, she prodded a little. "So you went to Mississippi and—"

"And I became a detective. There was an opening in the white-collar crime unit, so I took it."

"And now?" she asked.

"I'm definitely not sure dealing with white-collar crime is what I want to do for the rest of my life. I investigate CEOs, money laundering possibilities, and then I call in the appropriate acronym."

"Acronym?"

"Government agency. Tax evasion is IRS, money laundering can be IRS along with FBI, drugs or guns can come under the ATF."

"Alcohol, tobacco and firearms."

He nodded.

"So usually you don't see something to its finish?"

"Sometimes. Maybe that's what bothers me most. Maybe that's why I want to see this to its finish."

"I can certainly understand that." She took hold of his arm. "But, Nash, this is personal for you, too. It could cause you damage even though you don't think so now."

He wrapped her arm around his and started walking. "Don't worry about me, Cassie. I'll handle whatever comes my way. I've been taught to do that profession-ally, and I've learned to do it personally."

Cassie knew Nash believed what he was saying, but she still had her doubts. How could he put his biologi-cal father's wife in jail and not have regrets?

But she wasn't going to ask any more questions be-cause Nash was acting as if that discussion was over. That was his way of dealing with questions he didn't want to answer. Or maybe feelings that came up that he didn't want to feel. Even though she didn't know him well, she knew that. How was that even possible in two weeks?

She glanced at his profile, the jut of his jaw, the breadth of his shoulders. She wasn't sure. She just knew she was mightily attracted to him as she'd never been to another man.

They walked, paused and studied paintings. Cassie tried not to compare anything to her own work, but that was difficult not to do. "Some of these are so good," she murmured, studying a landscape of the Southwest with its red rocks, almost turquoise sky, cactus and many colors of earth.

"You've lost confidence, haven't you?" Nash noted.

"I don't know what you mean." She brushed off his words as if they were too far-fetched to consider.

"You know exactly what I mean. You don't think your work is as good as what's displayed here."

"How can I think anything else? They rejected my work."

"Oh, Cassie. You know that saying? Beauty is in the eye of the beholder?"

"Maybe."

They walked on, past booths from various galleries

that had displays. Cassie spotted Nash pocketing business cards from them. She didn't ask him why. Nash was an investigator. His job was to collect information, so maybe that was what he was doing. Who knew? She couldn't expect him to pour his heart out to her just because they'd shared a kiss...and a confidence.

She thought about their kiss again. Many more of those and they would know each other *very* well.

Pictures played in her mind that made her blush. She couldn't believe she was thinking about Nash in that way, imagining him without his T-shirt, fantasizing about running her fingers through his hair. She'd never had a crush on anybody, not even Cody Sinclair, who'd walked away because her mother had been deemed a criminal. This *wasn't* a crush on Nash, she scolded herself. This was just a woman's response to an attractive man. Completely natural.

When they'd walked around awhile longer, Nash said, "Have you looked at enough paintings?"

"Have you?" she returned.

He blew out a breath. "Another question doesn't answer a question."

"All right," Cassie said. "Tell me what you'd rather do instead of looking at paintings."

He narrowed his eyes at her. "You know, I think you could give a lawyer a run for his money."

She gave him a coy smile. "I have no idea what you mean."

He chuckled. "If you're ready to leave, why don't we stop at the tasting room at the Mendoza Winery? We can have a little fun, taste wine and bring a bottle back to the B&B. Do you have time for that?"

She'd like to thank Carlo again for arranging her

Paint and Sip social. Assuming he was there. She checked her watch. "I have time. I think that sounds like a great idea."

Although she didn't usually drink, tasting a few of Carlo's wines could be fun. She'd take a sip of each and that would be that.

Nash hung his arm around her shoulders and pulled her close. After he did, she could smell a hint of citrusy cologne and she liked it. She liked feeling his warmth.

Who was she kidding? She liked him.

Nash knew exactly why he'd asked Cassie to go to the tasting room with him. He wanted to spend more time with her away from the bed-and-breakfast. When she was there, it was as if she had a burden on her shoulders. Out and about she smiled more and laughed more. Maybe there was something about the bed-and-breakfast that reminded her of something else. Maybe if they spent more time together, she'd tell him.

This time at the tasting room they went in a different entrance than the one for the restaurant. The two of them faced a large rough-hewn wooden door.

Nash took hold of the brass handle and pulled the door open. It creaked and they stepped inside. There was a reception area with high vaulted ceilings with dark beams. Beyond that they could see a marble-topped tasting bar crowded with wine glasses and corked bottles. In the center of the room sat a wooden trestle table that must be used for the tastings.

A man in a black shirt and black pants stepped out of an office located down the hall to the right of the wine bar.

He smiled as he came toward them. "I'm Ricardo," he said. "Are you here for a tasting?"

"We are," Nash confirmed, his hand possessively resting in the small of Cassie's back. It seemed natural to touch her like that. She didn't shrug away so he supposed it was the right thing to do.

"Have a seat," Ricardo said.

"Is Carlo here?" Cassie asked.

Ricardo shook his head. "He's away for the day."

"Will you thank him again for me for hosting the Paint and Sip?"

"Surely, I will. Now tell me what kind of wine you prefer."

"Sweet," Cassie answered. "But I really only want a taste. I don't really drink often."

Nash gave her a surprised look. He leaned close and whispered in her ear, "If you don't drink, why did you want to come? Are you sure you want to stay?"

"I wanted to thank Carlo again. And I've never tried the Mendoza wines. A tasting is just that, a tasting. I'll have a sip or two of each one. We're good, Nash."

As he gazed into her eyes, he suspected they would be *very* good together. Had he hoped after a glass of wine or two she'd be receptive to his advances?

No. He'd already decided that shouldn't happen. That was why he'd stayed away from her this week.

Nash looked up at Ricardo. "I like dry."

"I'm sure I can satisfy both of your palates," Ricardo assured them with a wink. "Do you know anything about wines?" he asked.

"I know about types and some of the good years. But that's about it," Nash responded.

"That's more than most people know." Ricardo went

to the bar and chose two bottles. He brought them to the table with two wine glasses. "This is Sunny Days—a Chenin Blanc," he told Nash. "It's a dry white wine. It's not well-known by many consumers. For the lady, let's try Southwestern Comfort—a Muscat Blanc. It is also a white wine but a bit sweeter. It goes well with chocolate." Ricardo brought a plate of chocolate, a basket of crackers and dish of cheese to the table.

Nash swirled the wine around in his glass and then took a sip. He nodded to Ricardo that he liked it.

"Try yours," Ricardo directed Cassie. "Of course, you're going to have to try chocolate with it."

She swirled the wine in her glass as Nash had done and took a sip. The way she licked her lips afterward made Nash almost break out in a sweat.

"What do you think?" Nash asked.

She smiled. "I think my guests might enjoy having this on hand. Let me try it with the chocolate." She took one of the chocolates on the tray and bit into it. Her expression was so sensual Nash wanted to kiss her before she was even finished the bite.

"I'll take a bottle of this one," she said.

Ricardo laughed. "But you haven't tasted the red yet."

Next Ricardo brought out Desert Sunset for Cassie, which was a Syrah. He chose Rodeo Nights—a Cabernet Sauvignon—for Nash.

After Cassie sipped what was in her glass, she shook her head. "I prefer the first one."

"Do you want to try it again?" Ricardo asked.

"No, I don't need to."

He looked at Nash. "Anything else you'd like to taste?"

"No. I'll just finish up what I have here. I'll also take a bottle of the first one."

Ricardo looked from one of them to the other. "I'll go back to my office for a little while so you can relax and enjoy the rest of your wine and the snacks." He took his leave quickly.

Cassie exchanged a look with Nash. "I'm not sure what that was about."

"My guess is he thinks we want to be alone. That's not a bad idea, you know."

She took another piece of chocolate from the plate and popped it into her mouth. Then she brought her gaze back to his. "So we can enjoy the snacks?"

Nash leaned toward her, his lips not very far from hers. "Maybe I'd like to taste the wine you were drinking on your lips. Take a sip and we'll try it."

He didn't know if she'd do it. He'd practically ignored her all week trying to settle how she fit into his life... *if* she did. After today, he knew she did. If she did let him kiss her again, that meant she was open to more. Though more of what, he wasn't sure.

Cassie took a very small sip of wine and then turned back to him. He leaned toward her once again and met her lips, tasting the sweetness on her mouth. But the kiss itself was anything but sweet. He took her lips in a possessive kiss that quickly deepened, their tongues meeting, stroking, striving for more. He broke away before he couldn't stop something that shouldn't go on here.

He tried to treat it lightly. "It must be the wine. I feel dizzy."

But she wasn't smiling. "Nash, this isn't a good idea."

"The wine tasting, the kiss or being alone together?"

"Take your pick," she said sadly.

"Are you saying you don't want me to kiss you again?"

"No, I'm not saying that. I'm saying you *shouldn't* kiss me again."

"Because neither of us need those complications?"

She nodded.

"Maybe it doesn't have to be complicated. Maybe we can just enjoy being together."

"I don't know," she confessed.

"Can you tell me why you don't drink?"

"I'd rather not," she said.

He could easily see she didn't trust him. If she didn't trust, then she must have been betrayed by someone. There was a lot more to Cassie Calloway that he had to discover. Could he do it in another two weeks?

He was going to try.

Chapter Seven

That evening Cassie cleaned up after dinner. Her guests had gone out for the evening and so had Nash. He hadn't come to supper. She thought about that afternoon and the tasting room at the winery. Yes, she still felt the effects of Nash's kiss when she thought about it, but her real focus was on the questions he'd asked. *If you don't drink, why did you want to come?*

She wished she could tell him her mother was in jail for vehicular homicide. She wished she could tell him her mother had been an alcoholic and that was why she herself didn't drink.

Cassie was wiping her hands on a kitchen towel when someone knocked at the front door. Cassie knew who it was immediately. Renata Garcia always knocked even though Cassie had told her over and over she didn't have to.

Cassie hurried to the door so the older woman didn't have to wait on the porch. She opened the door wide and Renata stood there, a smile on her face, a black shawl around her shoulders.

"Are you busy?" Renata asked.

"No, I'm not. The guests ate and left and I've finished cleaning up. Come on in. Can I get you something? A cup of tea? Iced tea?"

"No, I just came over for a little conversation."

In other words, Renata was lonely. That was one of the reasons Cassie was planning a birthday party for her next Sunday. Cassie had invited all of Renata's friends. After conversations with a few of them, she'd realized they wanted to help by bringing casseroles, so it was turning into a covered-dish social.

The older woman followed Cassie to the sitting area, where she seated herself in a comfortable armchair, letting the shawl drop back.

"You had a busy day today," Renata said.

Cassie knew her neighbor watched the comings and goings from her porch. "I did. Breakfast with guests and then I was out for a bit."

"With that nice Mr. Tremont."

Cassie had been hoping Renata hadn't seen that. "Yes, we went to the arts festival at the Palmer Center."

"I used to enjoy that," Renata said, looking a little sad.

"I wasn't allowed to take photos inside but I have some of the grounds. Would you like to see them?"

"Yes, I would."

For the next fifteen minutes or so, Cassie sat on the arm of Renata's chair showing her the photos on her phone.

"You and Mr. Tremont didn't come back until late afternoon."

Cassie moved back to the sofa. "We stopped at the Mendoza Winery for a bit. I brought back a bottle of wine for my guests."

"I see. Has he made any moves yet?" Renata asked.

"Renata," Cassie said with exasperation.

"Just wondering. He's very nice. You look good together."

Still remembering their kiss, Cassie felt the blush rising from her neck to her cheeks. "He'll be leaving soon. He lives in Mississippi."

"Tell me something, Cassie. What if you really liked this man? What if you more than liked him? And if not him, someone else. Would you think about moving?"

"No," she said immediately. "I can't leave Austin." And the reason? She wouldn't desert her mother. Even though her mother wouldn't see Cassie now, there might be a time when she would.

"Maybe I will take a cup of tea," Renata said, eyeing Cassie thoughtfully.

"Coming right up. I even have homemade oatmeal cookies to go with it."

"Wonderful," Renata said.

But right at this moment Cassie didn't think anything was wonderful. She had too many questions rolling around her head…and no answers.

On Monday, Cassie sat beside Danny on the porch. Their lesson wasn't going well because he seemed distracted. There was only one thing to do about that.

She put a hand on his shoulder and he looked up at

her. "You aren't pleased with anything you've painted so far, are you?"

He shook his head. Then he looked down at his shoes and wouldn't make eye contact again.

"Danny, there's nothing wrong with that. If you only knew how many paintings I've started and didn't finish."

That brought his gaze back up to hers. "I'm supposed to finish everything I start."

Cassie suspected that that was what Danny's father had decreed. Finishing for the sake of finishing when you didn't love what you were doing wasn't necessarily in your best interest or in the art's best interest. Cassie took the canvas of a landscape Danny had been working on off the easel.

When she looked into his eyes, she saw disappointment that she was giving up on him. But she wasn't.

Turning to the table where she kept extra supplies, she picked up a sketch pad. Without hesitating, she tore out one of the eleven by fourteen sheets and placed it against a piece of cardboard on the easel. Instead of paints, she picked up a carrier of colored pencils from the table and set it next to Danny. "I'd like you to draw something for me. Do you think you can do that?"

"Sure," he said, some of his confidence returning. The reason for that? She'd given him hope.

"Would you rather do it on the easel or over on the table?"

"I think I'd rather do it on the table."

"No problem." She made a place for him at the table and he brought over the paper. "I'd like you to draw what's on your mind. Don't think about it too much. Just draw it."

Danny took her at her word. He picked a few colored pencils from the carrier, set them on the table and then started. He drew quickly as if he didn't want to think too long about what he was drawing. His mind fed his fingers, and Cassie quickly saw the picture that emerged.

When Danny had finished, he laid down his pencil and sat back in his chair.

In the center of the picture, he'd drawn a fence. His mother was on one side of the fence and his father was on the other.

"Do you mind if I show this to your mom?"

His expression was worried. "I don't want her to get mad."

"I don't believe she'll get mad. I think she wants to know what you're thinking."

"Okay," Danny agreed reluctantly. "Can I try working on that landscape again?"

She positioned the canvas on the easel and let him go at it. Fifteen minutes later, she heard the door to the bed-and-breakfast open and then close. Before Dorie could come into the screened-in porch, Cassie smiled at Danny and picked up the picture he'd drawn. "Just keep on painting. I want to talk to your mom for a few minutes."

She stepped out from the porch and quickly went into the kitchen. There she placed Danny's picture on the counter.

Dorie crossed to her. "What do you have there?"

"Something I think you should see. Danny couldn't concentrate and I asked him to draw what was on his mind. This is what he drew."

Dorie's expression became so sad Cassie wanted to put her arm around her. The mom admitted, "I know his dad's leaving has been hard on him. I don't know how to make it easier." Her voice caught and Cassie could see tears in her eyes.

"The best thing to do is to keep Danny drawing and talking. When he seems troubled, ask him to draw what he's thinking about. He might be able to express his feelings that way rather than in words." Cassie knew how she'd kept everything inside all those years when she'd tried to hide the fact that her mom was drinking. Especially when her mom had gone to prison, painting had saved her.

She'd been so involved with her conversation with Dorie, she hadn't heard Nash come in. All of a sudden, he was standing there with them. She wondered how much he'd heard.

He pointed to the porch. "Is it okay if I say hello to Danny?"

Once again Cassie realized how well Nash handled people.

"Actually, it would be great if you could keep him occupied for a few minutes," Dorie said. "I have something to discuss with Cassie."

"No problem," Nash said with a smile.

As soon as Nash disappeared into the sunporch and started chatting with her son, Dorie assured Cassie, "I'll try to do what you suggest. Maybe I'll get him a set of watercolor pencils and he can begin experimenting with those."

"That's a great idea. When he finishes a drawing or a painting, ask him if he'd like to talk about it. Just take your cues from him. I was an introvert as a child and I spoke through my paintings. Not many people saw them but at least I was able to express my feelings that way."

Dorie looked nervous for a moment and twisted the handle of her purse. "You're so good for Danny and you've helped us so much. I have a favor to ask."

Cassie couldn't imagine what was coming. She just nodded for Dorie to go ahead.

"Do you mind if I list you as a contact for Danny at school in case of emergency? Some days I'm in meetings and can't have my phone turned on. His father usually has his turned off at the office, too."

After Cassie thought about the responsibility she'd be taking on, she said, "Sure. That would be fine. I can't imagine it would happen very often. Danny's a good student, isn't he?"

"He is. But in case he suddenly gets sick or has an accident on the playground, that would help. You'll have to stop at the school and have your picture taken and get an official ID."

"I can do that," Cassie assured her.

Dorie impulsively gave her a hug. "Thank you so much. With the divorce, I feel as if all my support has been kicked out from under me. Couples we were friends with suddenly don't want just a wife hanging around. And my friends have kind of drifted away because I don't have time for them. When I'm not at work, I'm with Danny and that's the way it has to be right now."

"True friends will understand that. They'll be waiting when you're ready for friendship again."

"I hope you're right. But I do feel as if I've made a new friend in you."

"You have." It had been years since Cassie had a close friend. She had a feeling Dorie could be one.

* * *

As Nash sat in the armchair in the sitting area after he'd chatted with Danny and the boy's mother had finished her conversation with Cassie, he thought again about an idea that had been plaguing him all day. He had his laptop on the hassock and he wasn't sure he should do what he wanted to do. As he thought about his kisses with Cassie, he tried to put them in perspective. Still, he didn't seem to have perspective right now. He just knew he felt closer to Cassie than he'd felt to anyone in a long time. All day he'd been thinking about telling her the truth concerning why he was in Austin. Yes, he'd told her the truth, sort of, but not the importance of who he was going after and not the burden of it.

He heard Cassie walk Danny and his mom to the door. He heard their chitchat as Cassie encouraged Danny to draw what he felt. He imagined she'd told Dorie to listen to her son, ask a few questions and see if he'd open up.

In his work, Nash had seen again and again how divorce impacted kids. He also knew firsthand what it was like to grow up without a dad, to miss that strong presence that could make a boy feel secure and encouraged. He'd had to do that for himself. Maybe that was one of the reasons he'd become a cop.

Cassie broke into his thoughts. She walked in carrying glasses of sweet tea.

She handed him the glass. "When you came in you looked as if you could use this."

"Maybe this and something stronger," he said, drinking in the sight of her.

Her eyes widened a bit as she sat across from him in

the corner of the sofa. After a few sips of iced tea, she set her glass on a coaster on the coffee table.

He took a few gulping swallows and set his down, too.

"Do you want to explain why you need something stronger?" she asked.

There was more caring in her voice than curiosity, and that was what decided it for him. "I have something to tell you."

From the look in her eyes, he could tell she knew this was something serious.

"Should I be worried about what you're going to tell me?" she wanted to know.

"Are there any guests still in the house?" He didn't want to be overheard.

Now she looked almost afraid. "No. Why? No one's coming after you, are they? You didn't bring a gun in, did you?"

"No and no." He sat forward on his chair. "I want to tell you who I'm investigating. I want to tell you who I really am."

"You did that, didn't you?" She looked confused now, but then she frowned. "Have you been lying to me again? You're not a detective, either?"

"Oh, I'm a detective," he hurried to assure her. "I didn't tell you the name of the family I'm investigating. I didn't tell you that that name is mine, too."

"This is about your biological father?"

"Yes. The family I'm investigating is the Fortunes."

Slowly she rose from the sofa and came over to sit on the hassock in front of him. "*The* Fortunes?"

Relief filled Nash at actually letting the information

out. "Yes. Jerome Fortune, also known as Gerald Robinson, is my biological father."

"Oh my gosh, Nash. Everyone in Austin knows who Gerald Robinson is. I mean, how many children he fathered has been plastered all over the media."

"Not all of them," Nash determined. "Amazing, isn't it? He couldn't have done better if he was a sperm donor, though I guess in a way he was."

Cassie still appeared astonished. "And this is the man your mother was in love with?"

Nash grimaced. "One and the same. I think part of her still loves him. She says he's gotten a bad rap, and I know she blames a lot of his misbehavior on his wife. But he's responsible for his actions. Every man is."

Cassie nodded slowly as if agreeing with him.

"I'm not after Gerald Robinson, per se," he explained.

"You said you found a thread when you were investigating that led to his wife. *She's* the one you're after, right?"

Apparently Cassie had listened well when he'd confided in her. "It depends. There's fraud involved. I'm trying to follow the money trail."

"You mean like bank transactions?"

"I did that back in Mississippi and I'm trying to make more connections now from here—bank transactions, buying and selling stock, deposits in her accounts and withdrawals, too. I made copies of all that. When I was in Mississippi working on the case, my investigation led me to a Charlene Pickett. I thought something about her looked familiar. Then it came to me. Charlene Pickett and Charlotte Robinson looked an awful lot alike. I believe they're the same person. Let me show you." He turned his laptop toward Cassie. He had a split screen with a photo of Charlene on one side, and Charlotte on the other.

"Those photos *do* look like the same woman—a younger version and an older version," Cassie agreed.

"A substantial amount of money disappeared from a major bank. I connected that to Charlene Pickett. If Charlene, now Charlotte, used that money to fund Gerald's rise to fame, he could be guilty, too."

Cassie looked him squarely in the eye. "If you're undercover, why are you telling me this?"

"I have to be undercover from the Fortunes, but I don't want to be undercover with you."

"Oh, Nash." Her voice held the same longing that he felt.

She was leaning toward him and he was leaning toward her. But they were both aware of that laptop between them. He had work to do and shouldn't be distracted. He'd hoped that by telling Cassie the truth, he would put an end to his distraction. But he could see immediately he'd just created more of a bond between them.

She was looking worried and she asked, "Is something wrong? You're putting an awful lot of trust in me. Why?"

Wasn't that a good question? For now, he'd give her a relevant answer. "Because I think you can handle it. You're not involved in the investigation. If I don't have to hide anything around you, then I can be myself. I can relax in between research jaunts, and maybe be able to think more clearly. I have to find incontrovertible evidence against Charlotte, not supposition."

"You have a hard road ahead of yourself. The Fortunes have power and influence. Gerald Robinson is rich. He can buy anything he wants, probably *anybody* he wants. Men like that don't get prosecuted. If they do, they get out of it, and the same would go for his wife."

Cassie sounded a bit bitter, which wasn't like her at all. "I suppose that's true some of the time, but I'm trying to prevent Charlotte Robinson from hurting anybody again."

"I suppose that's what being prosecuted for a crime is all about," Cassie murmured.

That thought seemed to energize her. She gently pushed his laptop off her lap and onto the hassock. Then she went back to the sofa, grabbed her glass of iced tea and took a few sips. He saw her hand was shaking a bit. Had he scared her?

Still sitting forward on his chair, he closed his laptop and then he asked, "Should I have kept this to myself?"

She instantly answered his question. "No, Nash. No. I'm glad you told me. Really, I am. I just…" She sighed. "I'm just not sure what it means for us."

"I'm not, either," he admitted. "But I didn't want half-truths to stand between us."

She nodded as if she understood. He so wanted to scoop her up from that couch and carry her up to his bedroom. But the way she'd moved away, she obviously wasn't ready for that. He didn't know if *he* was. So he remembered the other reason he wanted to talk to her. "I just didn't want to tell you my secrets," he said with a smile. "Are you busy? Is there something you need to be doing right now?"

"Not at the moment," she concluded, giving him a smile of her own.

"The light is still decent. Would you like me to

take photos of your paintings? Since we both have the time—" He left the sentence open-ended. He wasn't about to force her to spend time with him, though he really wanted to do this for her. "If you want to stay down here I could do it on my own."

"No, I'll come to the attic with you. I can pull out the ones that I think have the most merit."

"They *all* have merit. Have you worked any more on the one on the easel?"

"A little. But it's not finished yet."

"And you wouldn't want me to take a photo of your best painting before it's finished."

"Exactly."

"My camera's in my room. I can stop there on the way."

Cassie was nervous as she waited for Nash in the attic. She felt honored that he'd trusted her with the real story behind his visit to Austin. On the other hand, she was scared. He was a cop first and foremost. Her mother had committed a crime, whether it was unintended or not. Cassie couldn't imagine he'd ever understand what had happened or her feelings for her mother, or the fact that she still loved her even though her mother wouldn't communicate with her. Her mother thought she was protecting Cassie, and maybe she was. Maybe Cassie didn't want to know about the reality of prison and her mother's life there. But she'd been without a father most of her life. She didn't want to lose her mother, too.

How could Nash understand any of that when his feelings about right and wrong were so solid? She remembered all too well how Cody had ended their relationship after he'd found out about her mother. Why should she take a chance on that kind of heartache again?

She heard the steps creak as Nash climbed them. When he appeared with his camera, she wondered if she should rethink this whole thing.

But she didn't get a chance to do that because he asked, "What do you want to start with?"

Concentrate on your paintings, she told herself.

"I'll just pick out a few," she said.

"Nonsense. We'll do them all, then you can decide which ones you want in your portfolio."

That made sense, but it would take longer. They'd be up here together for a while. Just the two of them. She could handle it. She'd just make sure she stayed at least three feet away from him at all times.

As she quickly thought about the best way to photograph her paintings, she suggested, "Let's do them in batches—landscapes, then animal paintings, then symbolic works."

"Sounds good."

His gaze locked to hers, and she decided maybe four feet between them might be better than three.

Turning away from him, she went toward the corner where her landscapes were located. He, of course, followed. She lifted first one, then the second, then the third and positioned them against the wall. It didn't take long for him to photograph each one.

He said, "I'll take two photos of each painting. That way, if one isn't exactly the way you'd like it, you'll have a choice."

Again, that sounded very reasonable.

Eventually they came to the last series of paintings. She turned around the hummingbird and butterflies and then the wildflowers. For these, instead of zooming in, he moved closer to each painting. As she turned the last one to reveal a gazebo with twinkle lights set against the backdrop of a full moon, he moved in again. They were only about a foot apart.

His voice was a bit husky when he told her, "I have a spare flash drive. I'll put together a file with the photos and you can have the drive. That way you can have them printed in whatever size you'd like."

He was watching her and she was watching him. The movement of his lips as he spoke was mesmerizing.

She cleared her throat. "I have a company that I send photos like that to. They do a good job."

"Terrific." He came even closer. Cassie was against the wall so she couldn't back up. She could scoot out around him, she supposed, but she didn't want to.

Nash was looking at her lips, his gaze intent and suddenly hungry. He moved and she anticipated his kiss. Instead, he bent to place the camera on the floor. She closed her eyes and let out the breath she was holding and that was when she felt it. The tingling sensation of his hand on her neck, sliding under her hair. Reflexively she turned her face up to his. As he came even closer, she could smell the lingering scent of aftershave. It was masculine and spicy, and she wondered if she opened her eyes what she would see in his. But the thought fled as she felt his breath on her lips.

Their other kisses had been fast and hot. She felt the heat now, too, but more than that, she felt Nash's sensuality meeting her own. After he kissed her cheek, he let his lips trail to her mouth. He was coaxing her into passion and she didn't need to be coaxed. She sighed and when she did, she could feel his tongue touch her lips. Although the kiss was slow, there was a rawness about it. When his lips finally took hers, she grabbed onto his shoulders and held on tight. Kissing Nash was all that mattered in the world.

She'd never felt such a disturbing desire to be one with someone, to be one with Nash. His arms were around her, and hers were around him. She slid her fingers into his hair and as the kiss went deeper, he groaned. They were both eager and hungry. She felt Nash's heat all around her, or maybe that was her own meeting his. Their tongues searched each other's mouths, and all Cassie thought about was both of them without clothes, in bed, doing what was coming so naturally to them. Maybe it was that picture that made her hesitate.

A small moan escaped her lips as she set her palms against his chest. When she opened her eyes, she thought he looked as dazed as she felt. She knew now that she was undoubtedly falling for him.

"You want to stop?" he asked in a gravelly voice.

"We have to." She knew she sounded a little desperate, but there it was. She wanted him, yet she knew she shouldn't want him.

Nash backed away. "That got more intense than I intended it to."

She simply nodded because she couldn't seem to find the words to speak.

"I think we're finished up here," he said with a wave at all the paintings.

"We are," she agreed.

He asked, "Do you want me to find another place to stay?"

She had to be honest with him. "No."

This time he nodded. "Are you coming downstairs?"

She took refuge in the talent she'd taken refuge in as a child. "No, I'm going to stay up here and paint awhile."

"Then I'll see you tomorrow," he said. "I'll give you the thumb drive then."

"Thank you, Nash. For everything." He'd made her feel like a woman again.

His smile was wry when he said, "No thanks necessary." Then he descended the steps onto the second floor.

Cassie had fully intended to paint, maybe to finish her work in progress. Instead she found herself reaching for her sketchbook and drawing the profile of Nash Fortune Tremont.

Chapter Eight

Maybe because Nash was chasing after the Fortunes most of the day, he looked forward to getting glimpses of Cassie, to eat with her and her guests, even to help her clean up the dishes. Most of the time they didn't talk much, but there was a connection between them. He certainly couldn't understand it.

Tonight as they were clearing the table, Cassie said to him, "Soon I'm going to have start paying you for helping me."

"No chance of that," he responded. "It's good for me to wind down this way."

"Tonight I especially appreciate the help."

"Do you have an art class?"

"No. A Chalk in the Park event for kids."

He'd seen the sign Cassie had hung at the front desk, but he hadn't known exactly what it meant. But anything she promoted had to be good for children and families.

"What's that all about?" he said, very curious about the event.

She stacked plates and added silverware on top of those. "The volunteers from the art center put containers of those big sticks of colored chalk at intervals on the sidewalks in the park. There's a volunteer at each station. The kids draw what they like on the pavement."

"While the volunteers make sure everything's kosher with no disturbing graffiti," Nash guessed.

"Exactly." She carried the dishes into the kitchen. "I knew I wouldn't get there until later tonight so I'm not taking one of the stations. But I'm going to help with general monitoring, and if any of the kids need any assistance, I'll be there."

"That sounds like something I could use right now. A night in the park with kids and colored chalk."

"You're not having any luck with your research?" She sorted the silverware and placed it in the dishwasher.

"That depends on what you mean by luck. Maybe I'm finding out *too* much."

"Anything specific?" Cassie asked.

He joined her in the kitchen. "You want to get going. You don't need to talk about this now."

"We don't need to talk about it at all if you don't want to."

Cassie broke eye contact and moved away from him to load the dishwasher. He didn't want her to think he was shutting her out. This time he wasn't. He followed her and placed his hand on her arm.

Turning toward him, she assured him, "I really don't mean to pry. But if you need a listening ear, I'm here.

I don't have to worry about being late because no one expects me at a specific time."

Nash took a towel from the counter and folded it in half. "I wanted to see how some of the Fortunes live. Not all of them are rich, and don't want to be from what I read. And I really had no intention of doing this." He stopped.

"Something to do with your biological father?"

"Yes. I went to his estate and parked down the street from the gate. And it *is* an estate, not just a property."

"I don't understand the difference."

"It's surrounded by a stone wall and has an electronic iron gate and a long winding driveway. According to aerial shots I've seen online, it actually looks like a Mediterranean castle."

"Stone walls and iron gates mean he wants to keep people out...or his wife does."

Cassie's suspicions were very much like his own. "I guess it makes sense if he's rich. He can have any kind of house he wants...any type of security he thinks he needs."

"I'm not sure anyone needs a house like that," Cassie decided.

"My investigative training taught me a lot about fishing around the internet. I found other aerial shots that showed multiple wings, a pool and a whole lot of trees that hid pretty much everything else."

Cassie admitted, "I've read several articles written about Gerald Robinson."

"There have been many articles written about him. In one, there's a photograph of him in his library, where there are rows and rows of books, and even a rolling ladder."

After studying him carefully, she asked, "Do you resent it all?"

"You mean the butler and the Persian rugs? Those were mentioned in one of the articles, too. I don't know if *resent* is the right word. I think he's a despicable man who doesn't deserve any of it. And if I'm right about his wife, she certainly doesn't deserve it, either. But I imagine she's done everything in her power to keep it."

"You said you saw a photograph of him. Do you see yourself in him?" Cassie asked softly as if the question might irk him.

"I saw some resemblance. Fortunately, I take after my mother."

Taking off her apron, she perceptively suggested, "With a house like that, it sounds as if he might be afraid of the outside world."

"You mean paparazzi finding out all of his business? Maybe how many more illegitimate children he has?"

"Possibly that," Cassie confirmed. "But maybe it's his way of having a quieter life inside. You can read all the articles in the world about him, Nash, but that doesn't mean you're going to know him from them."

She was so right about that. "Thank you," he said.

"For what?"

"For letting me vent a little."

"I think about ninety percent of that venting is still inside you. But you're welcome if it helped."

"I think what would help more is the kids and the chalk in the park…and you."

She looked flustered. "Me?"

"You're a breath of fresh air in my life right now, Cassie. I appreciate that more than you know."

She looked a bit embarrassed, as if compliments

were foreign to her. He couldn't imagine why. She was a beautiful woman.

"I have to go get dressed," she said. "Jeans and a T-shirt will be a better outfit for kneeling on the pavement and getting covered with chalk. I'll meet you down here in ten minutes?"

"Ten minutes is good. I'll be waiting."

A half hour later Nash had parked his SUV in a public lot and he and Cassie walked to the park. It was a beautiful night.

"Are there lights in the park if this goes on for a while?"

"Oh, yes. There's a gazebo in the middle and that's all lit up. There are gas lights down each of the sidewalks leading to the gazebo."

"Do parents stick around?"

"Some do and some don't. It depends on how old the kids are, and how much freedom they have on their own."

"If I were a parent, I'd want to be there. Even with volunteers, I wouldn't want to leave my kids in anybody else's hands." When he glanced at Cassie, he saw that she was looking at him. "What?"

"I believe you've seen a side of life that I haven't."

"That's true. I've seen kids getting hooked on drugs too soon. I've seen men approach kids who shouldn't be anywhere near them. I've broken up domestic fights because adults can't act like adults. So I don't see the world as a safe place."

Cassie was frowning now and he didn't have a chance to ask her about that. As they entered the park, a boy about eight years old came running toward her.

"Cassie, Cassie. Come see my drawing. Micah says it's terrific."

"Micah Hanson is one of the volunteers," Cassie explained. "Okay, Rodney. Let's go find him."

Nash followed her but he examined the chalk drawings on the sidewalk along the way. Some of them were quite good. Many of them were funny and he had to smile.

At least he smiled until they reached the volunteer who was packing more chalk into a container to place on the sidewalk. The man, who looked to be in his late twenties or early thirties, was dressed in shorts, sneakers and a T-shirt. He had black hair and snapping brown eyes that now focused on Cassie.

"Cassie, hey! It's good to see you."

She went right over to him as if they were close friends. "Hey, Micah. How's it going tonight? Is everybody behaving?"

"Except the volunteers," he said with a roll of his eyes. "One of the dads came with liquor on his breath and I told him to go back home. His wife was with him and she stayed instead with their little boy."

"Good job," Cassie said.

Nash didn't like the looks Micah was giving Cassie. They were definitely interested looks, and he wondered how much the two of them worked together.

Rodney was pointing to his chalk drawing behind Micah. "Come look, Cassie."

"Give me one minute," she told the little boy. "Micah, this is Nash Tremont. He's staying at the B&B. He thought he'd enjoy this adventure, too."

Nash extended his hand and Micah took it. But it definitely wasn't going to be the beginning of a beautiful friendship. He suddenly wanted to put his arm around Cassie and tell Micah, *She's mine.* But that thought didn't even belong in his head. They weren't at that stage yet.

Yet?

What was he thinking? He may care for Cassie, but it could never work. His life was in Mississippi and hers was here.

"Excuse me, guys," she said. "Rodney needs me."

Leaving the two men alone, she knelt on the ground beside Rodney without giving a second thought to what she was wearing. In no time at all, two more children had joined her, a little boy and a little girl. Cassie was asking them questions and coaxing them to draw. They did…in as many colors as there were sticks of chalk in the bucket.

Micah said to Nash, "She's good with the kids. They love her."

"What's not to love?" Nash asked before he thought better of it.

Micah narrowed his eyes. "How long are you staying at the B&B?"

"Awhile."

"Are you from around here?" Micah asked.

Nash suspected the man was feeling out his competition. Nash wished he could say he *was* Micah's competition. "No. I'm from Biloxi."

"A long way from home," Micah commented, probably just to make conversation.

"Business," Nash said as if that explained it all.

"I see."

Nash thought Micah looked relieved.

Claiming his home turf, Micah commented, "I'd better help Cassie. I think she needs reinforcements. She'll soon have a whole herd of kids around her."

Nash supposed that was true and with Micah helping her—

She didn't need a clash between male egos or Nash watching her closely to see if her interactions with Micah were familiar or friendly.

Seeing a bench nearby, he crossed to it and sat. He had photos of documents on his phone. He could scroll through them for a while, at least.

He purposely did not pay attention to Cassie, Micah and the children.

It wasn't long before he heard laughter. In spite of himself, he looked toward the kids and Cassie. Apparently, each child was explaining what they had drawn. They were sitting in a circle with Micah and Cassie, and Micah's hand was on Cassie's shoulder.

Friendly or familiar?

Nash stayed where he was.

Darkness had almost descended when the kids finally dispersed as their parents came to fetch them. By the light of one of the lanterns along the path, Nash noticed Micah give Cassie a hand up. Then they hugged. From what he could tell, they didn't kiss. He supposed that was good news.

Minutes later Cassie sat beside Nash on the bench. She didn't speak for a few heartbeats. Finally, she asked, "Why didn't you come over and join in?"

"I thought three adults might be a crowd," he said tersely.

Putting her hand on the back of the bench, she turned toward him and studied him for a long moment. "Are you talking about me and Micah?"

Nash shrugged as if it didn't matter to him. Yet his words belied the shrug. "You two looked like something's going on."

"Yes, something's going on," she answered with some heat. Nash's heart seemed to drop to his knees, but then she continued. "We work at the community center together, and we're friends."

"The two of you seemed a little chummy for just friends."

That comment had Cassie rising to her feet. "Are you ready to go? I have to make sure all my guests are tucked in for the night."

"Including me?" he asked, in what was supposed to be a teasing voice.

"Including you." Her voice *wasn't* teasing in return.

Their drive back to the bed-and-breakfast was quiet. Letting out a resigned sigh, he gripped the steering wheel tighter. He knew Cassie was annoyed with him so there just didn't seem to be any point pushing conversation. However, he wasn't the type to let things go, or to just let them simmer. Once they were inside and he saw no one else was around, he stopped at the counter in the kitchen and so did she.

"I'm going to get a glass of iced tea," he said. "Can I pour you one?"

When she looked about to refuse, he pulled two glasses from a tray on the counter and went to the refrigerator for the tea. He poured two glasses before she could say no. Then he set one in front of her.

"Are you sure you and Micah are only friends?" he asked. "When I was talking to him, something about him told me there was more."

"Maybe on *his* side," Cassie explained. "He asked

me out once but I said no. As I told you, my life is too busy to date."

He'd questioned many suspects in his career, and he easily saw through that excuse. There had to be some reason she didn't want to date, and soon he'd ferret it out.

Before she could turn away from him, or go to her room, he placed his hands on her shoulders. "I'm sorry I didn't join in with the spirit of fun tonight. But I can tell you why. I didn't like the idea that you and Micah might be involved."

"You were jealous?" The surprise in her voice almost coaxed him to smile.

He took a deep breath. "I'm not going that far." When he noticed her lips turned up a little, he asked, "Do you like the idea of me being jealous?"

Her smile broadened a bit. "I'm not sure. I can tell you one thing. I've never kissed Micah."

As he brought her closer to him, she didn't pull away. "That's good to know. Because I'd like to be the only one who's kissing you, at least for now."

As soon as his lips touched hers, he knew he'd felt more than jealousy tonight. They generated heat whenever they were together, and it was a heat that wasn't strictly physical. That was what puzzled him most of all. He'd sworn he'd never get emotionally close to a woman again, but it had happened faster than he'd ever realized it could. He was still fighting the idea of caring too much. When he had Cassie in his arms, he didn't think at all.

As he came up for air, he rubbed his jaw against her cheek. He knew there was a bit of stubble from his five-o'clock shadow, and he'd wondered how she'd like the sensation. She seemed to like it because she brought her hand to his cheek and rubbed it along his chin.

"Your stubble is sexy," she whispered.

All he wanted to do was sweep her up into his arms and make love to her anywhere they could find a place to land. Yet he didn't want to push what was happening between them for lots of reasons. A short-term affair sounded great in theory. But in the long run, he didn't think Cassie was that kind of woman. And for him—

He hadn't had a serious relationship for so long he wasn't sure he knew how.

Sliding his hands into her hair, he leaned back. "I think the two of us are becoming more than friends. I also believe we should both think about that before we act on it." He lowered his arms. "And that's why I'm going to go up to my room."

She looked flustered but she quickly motioned to the glasses on the counter. "You didn't drink your tea."

He picked up his glass. "I'll take it with me, along with the memory of that kiss."

As he walked toward the stairs, he could feel her gaze on his back burning right through his shirt. He had to ignore the heat until he could think about the whole thing rationally.

But he had the feeling that *rational* and *Cassie* didn't belong in the same sentence.

Storms rolled through Austin after midnight. Cassie had just fallen asleep. It had taken her a while because she'd been thinking about Nash. Maybe it was the thunder that had awakened her. As soon as she opened her eyes, she saw the bright flash of lightning at the windows. A loud crack made it sound as if lightning had hit something close by.

Usually she checked the weather before she went to bed each night in order to give a forecast to her guests by morning. But tonight, she'd been distracted. She hadn't thought about the weather forecast.

The wind howled against the house as rain pelted the window. She hoped the electricity didn't go out. Each room was equipped with a battery-powered lantern tucked into the closet. That detail was listed on the page of conveniences that was in the binder by the telephone in each room. She also had flameless candles and lanterns downstairs in case guests wandered down there because they couldn't sleep. Still, she hoped the power would stay on.

Cassie was debating about making a cup of tea when the wind blew with a roaring gust. There was a streak of lightning and a second later a crack of thunder. Along with that, she heard a crash that sounded as if it came from the screened-in porch. She jumped out of bed and ran toward the porch. Switching on the overhead light, she covered her mouth with her hand.

A large tree limb had crashed into one of the screens and torn it. The wind blew her coral cotton nightgown against her legs. But she was almost unmindful of it as she tried to assess the damage. Not only had the screen been torn, but the giant limb had damaged the frame.

Suddenly Nash was standing there beside her, chest bare, hair tousled, a sleepy expression on his face. "I was going to ask what that noise was, but I see I don't have to."

Cassie's hair was being tossed all about and rain was blowing in.

Nash took hold of Cassie's arm and tugged her out of the porch. Then he slid shut the sliding glass door. "You're getting wet," he told her.

For the first time, she realized her wet nightgown clung to her. She should be embarrassed but she wasn't. She was too worried about another expense. "I have to figure out how to fix the porch on my own. I really can't afford a repair bill."

Nash took her hand and turned her to face him. "Cassie, it's not that bad. It's an easy fix."

"I suppose I can find a video on YouTube to tell me how. I'm just not sure what to do about the frame."

"I can fix it for you."

Now Cassie looked at Nash, really looked at him. His beard stubble, darker than it had been last night, was so sexy. Then there were his muscled broad shoulders, his strong arms, the brown chest hair that sprinkled his chest.

She swallowed hard. "I can't let you do that."

"Of course you can. I worked construction a couple of summers. I know how to do it. I promise. If you feel you have to help, you can paint the frame after I put it together. After a trip to the hardware store, a couple of hours ought to do it."

"I can't let you spend your time on this," she insisted.

They were standing practically nose to nose and she could feel his body heat. He could probably feel hers, too. Her nightgown wasn't much of a covering anymore as it clung to her breasts, to her waist, to her hips and legs. But to her amazement, Nash kept his gaze on her face.

"You have to learn how to accept help," he scolded.

"I know how to accept help," she said almost indignantly. "I just don't want to be beholden to anybody."

He cocked his head as if he was wondering why, and she was afraid he might ask the question. She knew better than to be indebted to anybody. She didn't want to owe them because she couldn't reciprocate.

She once had friends who she thought cared. She went to their houses and had supper with their families. Real families. They would watch movies and eat popcorn together. The problem was she'd never invited them to her house, or rather her mother's apartment. The main reason—her mother was usually drunk by the end of the day.

Her mother's disease had been a well-kept secret, at least from Cassie's friends. If their parents knew about it, they never mentioned it. Her mother was good about her drinking, if anything could be good about it. She took in sewing. She tried to do that or errands in the morning so she could bring in a little bit of money and keep the grocery clerk from seeing her swaying. The post office clerk wouldn't hear slurred words. But by early evening she was slurring, weaving and even blacking out. Cassie hadn't known whom to turn to for help. She'd thought about telling one of her teachers but what if that had gotten her mother into trouble? What if they had taken Cassie from her and put her in some strange house somewhere? At least her mother cared about her.

But because Cassie hadn't gotten her help, the inevitable had happened. The most horrific thing had happened. Her mother had run a red light, smashed into another driver and killed him. It was Cassie's fault she was in jail for vehicular homicide.

Nash gently swiped dampness from her cheek.

"Where did you go?" he asked. "Those looked like some heavy thoughts going through your head."

Her throat was tight and her chest felt so heavy. She couldn't return a light comment or shrug off the question. Not about this. Not right now. She remembered how after the accident all of her friends had ignored her, how she hadn't received any more invitations to their homes. Thank goodness she'd been twenty-one so nobody could place her anywhere she didn't want to be.

Her mind quickly swept over their conversation, and the present became more important than the past. Nash standing in front of her practically naked—well at least half of him was—was more important than any relationship she'd ever had with a man. She had to tell him something that was true.

"When I went to college, I had three part-time jobs. I'd received a scholarship but I still had to pay living expenses. There wasn't anybody to help me. I'm used to making my own way. I found out when people gave me something, they expected something back. Sometimes I couldn't give it."

"Are you talking about men?"

"Not just men. I learned to pay my own way, keep my own counsel and be my own person. So here's the deal. If you repair the porch, I'll comp you three nights."

"That sounds more than fair," he agreed. "We can go to a hardware store tomorrow and get supplies."

"There's an independent hardware store that I use. He always gives me good prices. He's fair, and I'd like to see his business keep on thriving."

"Independent stores are having a hard time of it these days."

She nodded. "They are."

Cassie could still hear the sound of rain beating against the house, though the lightning and thunder had died away. She was about to escape to her room when Nash said, "But I'm not thinking about small businesses right now. Are you?"

Standing here like this, so close to him, all she could think about was touching him.

"What are you thinking?" he asked her.

"That you look mighty good without a shirt."

The corners of his lips turned up. But in his eyes, she saw a smoldering passion that seemed to be all for her.

"And you look mighty good in that color," he said with a straight face.

Her voice was husky when she responded, "I'm sure your eyes are just on the color."

"I'm trying hard," Nash joked.

As Cassie had remembered past years with her mom, tension had strung her body. But now that tension faded away. Tonight, she was here with Nash. Maybe, just maybe, she shouldn't think so hard about what was right and what was wrong, what was proper and what wasn't. Nash leaned in and kissed her forehead. When he backed away, she found her hands going to his chest almost of their own accord.

Nash enclosed her hands in his. "Not a good idea if we're not going to spend the night together."

"But I…" Cassie began.

He cut in, "You're still not sure. If we sleep together, I want you to be very sure. I'm not one of those men who will repair your porch and expect something in return. Everything about us has to be no strings, Cassie."

"No strings," she repeated, knowing in some ways that was how she'd lived her life.

Releasing her hands, he ran his thumb over her lips. "One kiss would lead to another and another and another. When that happens, I want us both to be on the same page."

Slightly embarrassed, overwhelmed by the desire to have Nash kiss her, she said, "Good night, Nash." Then she turned and walked to her bedroom. She was pretty sure as she did, he wasn't just noticing the color of her nightgown.

Chapter Nine

When Cassie awakened the next morning, she remembered changing her nightgown from last night. It had been damp and Nash had...

She was up at daybreak for a very good reason. She was sure the storm had left debris on the property and she needed to clean it up before the guests awakened. Breakfast would be an easy one this morning—omelets—so she could spend the next hour doing what she had to do.

After she showered and dressed, she went to the porch to examine it in the daylight. The sun was just streaking over the horizon, turning the sky fuchsia, orange and gold. It was in her eyes until she opened the sliding glass door and stepped onto the porch. There, to her surprise, Nash was already working. He had lugged the tree limb into the yard. He'd also stacked loose limbs and slight branches in a pile. Her backyard was cleaned up.

"I'll have to comp you another night," she said.

"Don't you dare." He shook his finger at her. "I needed physical labor since I can't work out like I usually do."

"At a gym?" she asked.

"I just do weights at my place. It's faster and easier. In my line of work, I don't punch a clock. I might be at my office overnight. That's a cop's life."

She supposed it was. "I bet your mother worries about you constantly."

"Not so much since I moved to Mississippi and have been investigating white-collar crimes. She tells me she sleeps much better at night." He shrugged. "Do you have a saw?" he asked.

"I do." She pointed to the rear of the yard. "See that shed? It has a padlock. The combination is eight-two-three, right, left, right."

"By the time I finish cutting up these limbs, it should be time for breakfast."

"Omelets this morning. What's your passion?" As soon as she said it, she knew she shouldn't have.

"I'll tell you about my passion another time when we're alone. As for omelets, I like peppers, onions and hot sauce."

"Coming right up," she said with a laugh. "If you can eat that first thing in the morning, you can eat anything anytime."

He wiggled his brows at her. "Including chocolate-covered strawberries at sunset."

Was he hinting that that was something they could do together? She could imagine the chocolate, the sweetness of the strawberries, feeding them to each other. Then she could imagine kissing Nash.

To avoid those thoughts, she said, "The hardware store opens at nine. Do you want to go this morning?"

"Meet you at nine if all your guests have finished with breakfast by then."

Her guests *had* finished by nine and she'd cleaned up. Including Nash, she had four guests right now—a couple and a young woman from Tennessee who was visiting relatives. She was hoping that by summer, reservations would pick up and all of her rooms would be filled.

Cassie was getting used to riding with Nash now in his SUV. She climbed in and fastened her seat belt. After he was inside, too, and had started the engine, she pointed to the GPS. "Does that really get you where you want to go?"

"Most of the time," he said with a smile. "Why? Doesn't your car have one?"

"No, I have an older car. People I run into and the parents of the kids I teach tell me I should have one. But I don't travel that much so it seems like an expense I don't need."

"That depends on how good you are at reading paper maps or downloading directions from the internet."

"I suppose if I ever take a long trip I'd think about it."

The hardware store was less than a mile away and they were there and parked in no time. Cassie led Nash inside. She waved to Phil Lebeau, who was the owner. Phil was stocking shelves with faucets and fixtures, so she didn't bother him.

Nash led her to the back of the store, where he found

the wood he needed for the frame. Then he pulled out a roll of screening.

"I can carry that," she said.

"Why don't you take the wood strips. They're lighter."

She frowned at him. "I'm stronger than I look."

He laughed. "Next time I'll let you carry whatever's heaviest."

Next time. She liked the idea of having a next time with Nash, but she knew she shouldn't get too attached to the thought.

"Do you have a good hammer?" he asked her.

"I do, and a set of screwdrivers and wrenches. I'm well prepared."

He dipped his Stetson to her. "I should have known."

After they had pieces of wood cut and brought everything up to the cash register, Phil came over to check them out.

After Cassie made introductions, Phil asked, "So you're not helping her paint more rooms odd colors of paint?"

"What do you mean *odd*?" Cassie asked with a smile.

"Lime green and that coral color aren't my cup of tea," Phil grumbled.

"Have you ever seen the house?" Nash asked.

Phil shook his head. "Never have."

"I don't know how, but it all works. Her colors, furnishings and that mural all just tie in well together."

"I suppose so or she wouldn't have any repeat business." Phil narrowed his eyes at Cassie. "You've never brought a beau along with you before." He gave her a wink.

"He's just a guest at the bed-and-breakfast," she explained once more.

"A guest is going to help you make repairs?"

In a confidential tone Nash said to Phil, "She's comping me a couple of nights."

"Oh, I see," Phil said with a knowing smile, and Cassie knew she turned a bright shade of pink.

Nash hooked his arm around her shoulders. "Cassie tells me she's good with a hammer. I might let her help me."

Phil laughed and bagged the smaller items they'd bought. "That house needed mostly cosmetic changes, and Cassie did them all herself. I've got to give her credit for that, no matter what color paint she used."

After they checked out and were in the car once more, Nash turned to Cassie. "Why haven't you ever taken a beau into the hardware store?"

"I didn't do that this time," she retorted.

"I think since we've kissed, I could be considered your beau. And we *did* have lunch together. That could have been considered a date."

"What did *you* consider it?" she asked softly.

"I consider our kisses very hot, and indicative of further exploration."

Cassie rolled her eyes. "That didn't answer my question."

"And you didn't answer mine."

"I did answer you before. I told you I'm too busy to even think about a relationship."

She could see Nash wasn't buying that, and she didn't want to lie. "All right," she said. "I had a relationship a few years ago, but it ended badly. I haven't wanted to take a chance since then."

"Did you break it off or did he?"

She was about to tell him that was a very personal question when she remembered what he'd told her about his family. "He broke it off," she said, still feeling humiliated by the idea and why it had happened. As soon as she'd told Cody her mother was in prison, he'd turned tail and run.

"He was a fool," Nash said.

Cassie appreciated the compliment but Nash didn't really know her. If he really knew her, he'd leave before his time at the B&B was up. She was sure of it.

Back at the B&B, Cassie helped Nash carry everything inside and out to the porch. Her guests were out and about, so noise wouldn't bother them.

Nash said, "I want to lay the boards out and mark them before I start. I had the pieces of wood cut according to the sizes I needed, but if for some reason we got it wrong, I want to know now."

Cassie could see Nash was as precise about this as he was with everything else. Cut-and-dried, black-and-white, practical and precise. He was a cop, after all.

Nash had been working about an hour and she'd been doing laundry, when the phone rang. Hurrying to the kitchen she picked up the cordless phone there. Caller ID said the call was from out of area. She often got calls like that for reservations.

"Hello," she said cheerfully. "This is the Bluebonnet Bed-and-Breakfast. May I help you?"

"I hope you can. My name is Marybeth Tremont. My son isn't answering his cell phone and he gave me this number in case I couldn't contact him on the cell."

Cassie introduced herself, then assured the woman.

"Nash is doing repair work for me, so he might have his phone turned off."

"Repair work? Did you have some of those storms that came up through Texas to Oklahoma last night?"

"We did. A large tree limb crashed through the screen on my porch."

"Oh my," Marybeth said. "We had a bit of hail but I didn't have any damage, thank goodness." She seemed to hesitate a moment before she asked, "So Nash is doing the repair work for you?"

"Your son is a man of many talents. But then, a police detective has to be, I suppose."

"So he told you about that, did he?"

"He did." Cassie wasn't going to go into exactly what Nash had told her because she wasn't sure how much his mother knew.

"His work comes before everything," Marybeth said with a sigh. "I certainly wish he could come home more. I miss him. I miss the days when he'd talk my ear off about sports and school and anything else that came into his head. He got quieter as he got older."

"Maybe that had something to do with his work, too," Cassie suggested.

"You're probably right." The woman hesitated a moment, then said, "I don't want to take up too much of your time. Would you give Nash the message to call me?"

For some reason Cassie had the feeling that Nash's mother was really missing him right now. "No need for that. I'll get him. Just hang on."

Cassie took the cordless phone out to the porch, where Nash was unrolling the screen. "It's your mom."

With an arched brow, Nash took the phone. Cassie

left him alone on the porch so he'd have some privacy. She was in the kitchen about ten minutes later when he brought the phone back inside.

"I did have my cell turned off," he said. "I didn't want an interruption while I was hammering and measuring."

Cassie wasn't sure how to broach the subject she wanted to discuss, so she started with an easy comment. "Your mother sounds very nice."

"Oh, she is. I've always told her she should have been a Southern belle. She always tries to be so tactful. Midwesterners are blunter."

Cassie laughed. "I think that has more to do with personality than the part of the country where you were born."

"Maybe so. Did she talk your ear off?"

"No, of course not. But I do think she misses you. Maybe you could take time to go home and visit her."

He was already shaking his head. "You don't understand my life. Work comes first."

Before Cassie could stifle the words, she said, "Work will always be there, but you won't have your mother forever."

Nash didn't respond to that, but his lips tightened and his jaw became a little firmer. "I just have to fit the screen and put the panel in place. I should be done in fifteen or twenty minutes."

"You can just leave the tools and remnants on the porch. I'll clean up after you're finished."

"I finish what I start," Nash said, then headed for the porch.

Cassie considered their conversation as she went

into the laundry room. She was folding sheets when Nash came by and stood in the doorway.

He asked, "Need help with that?"

She just gave a little shrug. He must have taken that for assent because he took hold of the two ends of the queen-size sheet and brought it up to meet hers. Their hands brushed. Cassie's gaze went to his, then she quickly looked away, folding the sheet again and again. She laid it in the wash basket.

"I thought about what you said," Nash told her, "and you're right. I should get home to visit Mom more."

He had her attention now.

"But there's a reason I left Oklahoma and there's a reason why I don't go back and visit more."

"And that is?" she prompted. She couldn't expect him to answer her, but she thought she'd try anyway. He took a few steps toward her.

"I grew up in a small town where everybody knows everybody."

"So did I," she admitted.

"So you understand how everyone knows everybody's business. If something happens in a family, it's like an announcement goes out to the whole town. If it's not in the small newspaper, it's on people's lips when they meet at the coffee shop or see each other at the family restaurant."

She wished she could take Nash's arm or his hand or give him a hug because he looked as if this was very hard for him to say.

He continued with, "People heard my mom had had an affair with a married man, an outsider. Those who knew her realized she did it for love. But others who didn't know her as well figured she was out to get something that she couldn't get in other ways."

"You mean they thought she was looking for a sugar daddy?"

"Yes. Exactly. Which *wasn't* the case. So I heard rumors when I was growing up. My mom told me the truth when I was six or seven, and she told it in stages. I probably became a cop because there was some authority in that, a *don't-you-mess-with-me* message."

Because everyone is at least a little afraid of law enforcement? Cassie wondered. She knew how afraid of law enforcement she'd been when they'd come to collect her mother.

"I had a girlfriend on and off during high school," Nash went on. "She didn't seem to care what anybody else thought of me. I liked that about her."

"I imagine she was pretty, too."

Nash sighed and answered, "Yes, she was. After high school, we kind of went our separate ways. I went to the police academy and she went off to college. She was earning a business degree so she could be her dad's office manager. He ran a carpet and tile home improvement store."

"And because it was a small town, you knew when she returned."

"I did. But we didn't reconnect again until a couple of years later. Her father was mugged on the way to the bank to make a deposit. I was sent to the scene."

"So you reconnected."

He nodded, but his lips tightened. A moment later he admitted, "We did. I went to work finding the kid who did it, and together we helped her dad overcome the effects of the mugging. I celebrated with her and her family the night the perp was caught. Right after that, she and I started dating again. When I turned twenty-six, we'd been dating for two years, and I had made assumptions during those two years. I expected we'd get engaged, be married and have a family. Something about turning twenty-six just clicked with me. I wanted something solid, not like what my mother had had. I had a job, though the hours could be crazy. I also had money in the bank from overtime and from security work."

"You were ready," Cassie acknowledged, thinking Nash must have always been mature for his age.

"I was ready and I thought she was, too. I bought a ring. When I gave it to her, I didn't see the happiness on her face that I expected to see."

From the lines etching deeper around Nash's eyes and mouth, Cassie could see the emotional toll his story was taking on him. But this time she didn't say anything, she just waited.

"The bottom line was that Sara didn't want to marry a cop. She didn't want to worry every time I left for a shift. She didn't want to settle down with me and not have a real life because of my crazy hours. It turns out during those hours, she was dating someone else in nearby Norman. He was a college professor."

"Oh, Nash, I'm so sorry."

He shook his head and waved his hand as if he didn't want her sympathy or pity. "I was a fool. I was blind. I hadn't read any of the signs. Because of that, I knew I wasn't husband material and realized I had to up my professional game. I decided to change my life. I moved to Mississippi and became an investigator for white-collar crimes."

"And you don't go back to Oklahoma because the memories are just too painful."

"And I don't want to go backward. I want to move forward."

"But aren't you going backward investigating your biological dad and his wife?"

"I don't see it that way."

"Then how do you see it?"

"I see it as trying to right a wrong. If Charlotte did what I think she did, she deserves jail time."

"What if your biological father was involved?"

"Then he does, too."

Cassie was dubious and shook her head. "I still think you'll regret it."

"I'll find out, won't I?"

Somehow she and Nash had stepped closer to each other. She caught the scent of his aftershave, sweat, the essence of everything male.

Nash gazed steadily at Cassie. "This conversation got way too serious," he decided. "I think we both need fun in our lives."

"And how do you suppose we find that fun?"

"I've been searching sites in Austin and I found what looks to be a great zoo. I think we should go."

That wasn't at all what Cassie had suspected he'd suggest, but maybe it was a good idea. "Tomorrow?" she asked.

"You're on."

When Cassie and Nash emerged from the zoo office and headed for the timber-lined gravel path, she told him, "This zoo is one of Austin's best-kept secrets. Wait until you see the tigers' play area."

"Play area?"

"Yep. You know how household cats have those condos and cat trees that go to the ceiling?"

"I'm not real familiar with the concept," Nash said with a grin.

"Maybe I could explain it better if I told you that it's like a kid's jungle gym. The tiger can go from one level to the other and play or sun himself. In fact, do you mind if we head toward the wolves, and bears, and tigers and lions?"

"You sound excited." He took her hand in his as they walked along the path.

"Oh, look! Look at the peacock." She pointed to the bird that walked not ten feet from them.

"They're not in cages," Nash said as if they should be.

"Aren't they beautiful?"

When he didn't answer, she turned to him and saw he was looking at her. His eyes dipped down, and she felt as if he was taking in every inch of her, from her sneakers to her lime green shorts, yellow blouse and colorful, beaded necklace.

"*You're* beautiful," he said, capturing her gaze again.

She might have given a little gasp, she wasn't sure.

"Why do you look so surprised?" he asked. "You *are* beautiful. Don't you know that?"

"I don't think of myself like that. I'm just like any other woman trying to make my way, make a living, follow my dreams."

"Well, it becomes you." He squeezed her hand a little tighter. This feeling she had whenever she was with Nash always took her by surprise. It was a giddiness that seemed to infuse her whole body.

They walked for a long while without speaking, stopping often, enjoying the antics of all the animals. Soon they were at the exhibit of hybrid wolves. The sign read *FRISKY—Husky Wolf Mix*. "One thing I like best about this zoo is that they rescue animals who've been neglected. Somebody probably found this guy as a cub. But as he grew they realized he's more wolf than husky. I'm glad he's found a home." Maybe she liked this zoo so much because she felt a kinship with the animals who'd been rescued. The difference was that she'd rescued herself.

"I like watching the animal population," Nash said as he observed the wolf. "It can give an insight into human behavior. Sometimes I think the animals have it right and the humans don't. In fact, sometimes, I *prefer* the animal population. My buddy Dave's dog is so good with his kids, and he's loyal."

"What kind of dog is he?"

"A yellow Lab. When I'm around him, I can forget about what I've seen on the job. I've seen things on the streets I never want to see again."

This time Cassie squeezed *his* hand. He let go and curled his arm around her waist. As they continued walking, Cassie felt closer to him than she'd ever felt to any human being. How was that even possible, she wondered, given that she hadn't known him that long.

How close would you be if you told him the truth about your life?

Unable to ignore that voice in her head, she thought about her mother in prison. Her mom had tried detoxing several times over the years, but she'd never been successful. She'd needed something to live for other than a drink to get through the next few hours. Cassie had never been able to help her. She hoped her mother had gotten help now.

Deciding to dip her toe into dangerous waters, Cassie suggested, "Maybe criminals are like these animals. They need to be rescued and rehabilitated."

Nash shot a quick glance at her. "The difference between animals and humans is that humans have intelligence. That's why if someone commits a crime, they need to suffer the consequences."

"But if we could rehabilitate instead of incarcerate—"

"There are cages here, Cassie, for a reason. The same reason there are jails for people. The truth is, states and counties don't have enough money, resources or volunteers to even think about rehabilitation instead of incarceration. Jail isn't a solution but at least it gets criminals off the streets."

Cassie pulled away from Nash, using the obvious excuse of wanting to get closer to the next enclosure. She had no doubt now that Nash would back away from her completely if he knew about her mother. She'd been entertaining a dream that she should have known was as elusive as smoke.

Swallowing the bitter disappointment, she walked from exhibit to exhibit, forcing herself to enjoy the day. She genuinely loved seeing the animals and the wonder on children's faces as they observed the creatures.

"Look at that little boy," she said, pointing to a child who walked up to the tiger enclosure beside them. "No matter how many tigers he sees in a book, it can never prepare him for the reality of the real thing." She pointed to a white Bengal tiger. "They're my favorite," she said. "They're endangered. It's such a shame."

"You care about everything, don't you?" Nash asked, studying her.

"I don't know what you mean."

"Most people go through life letting the majority of what they see and hear slide by them almost as if it didn't exist. But you're not like that, not about humans or animals. You're in the present most of the time and it's such a good thing."

Cassie had always had to live in the present because she'd never known what to expect next. She could come home one day to an empty apartment. She could come home the next with her mother drunk as a skunk. And then there was the odd night when her mom would be sober. Then she'd talk to Cassie like any mother would, asking if she wanted to invite friends over. That wasn't something Cassie could ever do because her mother was too volatile, too unpredictable, too enamored with a bottle of whiskey instead of her daughter. Maybe Cassie cared so much about everything because her mother had seemed to care about nothing. She wished she could say that to Nash, but of course, she couldn't.

"I guess I live in the present so I don't worry so much about the future, and I don't think about the past."

"It seems like I'm always thinking about the past or the future," Nash admitted. "Even when I'm chasing down a witness, I think about what his testimony will mean in the future. And as far as the past goes, I suppose I never realized how it affected me until you said I should see my mom more."

"I didn't mean to criticize."

"No, you were thinking about her. In a way, I was punishing my mom because of my memories of Sara. How stupid is that?"

Turning toward him, Cassie said fervently, "You're anything but stupid. Life is like this path we're walking on with twists and turns that we never expect. We make our way the best we can and hopefully we learn as we go. I guess that's the secret for being successful in life, learning as you go."

Cassie pointed to a magnificent male lion sleeping in the sun in the adjacent exhibit. At least she thought he was sleeping until he became aware of them, opened his eyes and yawned, exposing all of his huge sharp teeth. Then he stood, showing off the majestic creature he was.

"Now that guy has a confident attitude," Nash joked. "And probably a roar to match."

When Cassie laughed, Nash encircled her with his arm again. This time she didn't pull away. This time she was just going to enjoy the moment because that might be all she'd ever have with Nash.

Chapter Ten

In the afternoon the following day, Nash established photo files with Cassie's paintings. As he thought about their trip to the zoo and everything they'd talked about, he decided he wanted to do something for her. They'd had fun together, enjoying all the animals. There were the animals you just looked at, but then there were some you could feed, like the goats and the llamas. They'd laughed a lot as they'd done that.

Beside his laptop on the desk in his room, he'd laid out the business cards he'd picked up at the arts festival. He'd pocketed about ten of them. He remembered what Cassie had said—that her paintings weren't good enough. That was a bunch of hogwash. He didn't know who the judges had been who had decided that, but he imagined everybody had different opinions. The same would be true for the gallery owners. Maybe, just maybe, she could score with one of them.

The first thing he did was compose a letter. He did it in his own name, acting as her agent. Then he attached the file. He made sure he wrote each letter individually so it had a personal touch. When he was finished, he sat back and felt as if he'd accomplished something.

As opposed to all his research on the Fortunes in the last three weeks?

He had to admit, all that work hadn't gotten him far. Maybe he would have to consider how he could speak to a Fortune incognito. But that would happen only as a last resort.

He decided to go downstairs for cookies and coffee. As he did, he heard the ringtone on Cassie's cell phone. He was familiar with the ding-dong ring now.

He heard her answer. As he went to the coffee urn and filled a mug, he recognized the strain in her voice. "Yes, that's right. His mother added me as a contact, and yes, I can pick him up."

Nash grabbed a napkin and stacked three oatmeal cookies on it. Anything Cassie baked was good and he had no doubt these would be, too. He listened to her phone conversation again.

"He was in a fight? That's not like Danny at all." She checked her watch. "I can be there in about twenty minutes." Again she listened for a few beats. "Yes, I'll stop at the desk and show my ID. He'll be in your office? I'll be there as soon as I can."

After she ended the call, she looked over at Nash. "Danny's mom asked me if she could add me as an emergency contact at Danny's school. Apparently, she has meetings when she has to turn her phone off, and

Danny's dad doesn't answer his cell phone when he's in court. When the school couldn't reach either of them, they called me. Danny got into a fight at school. They, of course, want to conference with his parents but they think it's best for Danny to leave the premises for now."

"You say this isn't like him?"

"Absolutely not. He's not the least bit aggressive and not even assertive enough. His mother brought him to me for lessons, hoping that his art could bring him out of his shell."

"Sometimes the quiet ones are keeping the most anger hidden."

"Maybe so, but I've got to get going."

"Is there anything I can do to help?"

"If any of the guests come back, just have them sign in that they're back. And could you answer the landline if it rings? I don't want to miss a chance at a reservation."

"I can do that. I know you're in a hurry, but drive carefully."

She gazed at him with soft, brown eyes that seemed to wake up every part of him that had been frozen, or maybe asleep. That included his heart and soul.

"Thank you," she said as she took her purse from a drawer in the kitchen, dropped her phone into it and hurried out the door.

About an hour later, Cassie entered the bed-and-breakfast with Danny. Beside her, the boy was sullen, his eyes cast downward to the floor.

"Danny, go over there to the sitting area and get yourself some cookies. I'll bring a glass of milk over. I think we should talk, don't you?"

The boy shrugged his shoulders and went to the table where the jar of cookies stood.

Nash was in the kitchen when Cassie went for the milk. She kept her voice low when she said, "He wouldn't talk to me about it. He kept silent the whole ride back. The nurse put that bandage above his eye. The principal said it was a surface scratch."

"Do you think we should just leave him to himself until his mom or dad gets here?"

"I called his mother and left a voice message that he was here. I texted her, too."

"Do you know what happened?"

"Not really. I'd like Danny to tell me himself if he will."

"Do you want me to sit in?"

"I don't think it will hurt. If I can't get him to talk, maybe you can."

Cassie carried Danny's glass of milk to him. He'd picked up two cookies but they were sitting on the occasional table beside him. Cassie sat beside Nash on the sofa across from Danny, who had seated himself in an armchair. "I left a message for your mom that you're here. I didn't want her to worry."

"She worries a lot," Danny mumbled.

"I'll bet she doesn't usually worry about you when you're in school."

Then he gave another shrug.

"Do you want to tell me what happened?" Cassie asked.

"No," Danny said solemnly.

Nash sat forward a bit. "Danny, you know that explanation's not going to work with your mom. You could practice on us."

Danny looked at them and blurted, "I'm never paint-ing again."

Cassie was shocked by that idea. "What do you mean you're not going to paint again? You have talent, Danny. I'd like to see you paint more, not less."

Nash had an understanding expression on his face. "Do you have a favorite sport?" he asked Danny.

"I like to watch basketball."

"I like to watch baseball. I dreamed about being a major leaguer someday."

"You were that good?" Danny asked.

Nash laughed. "Not at the beginning. I was never a major leaguer, not even close. But I did win a few games for my team."

"What position?" Danny asked.

"Pitcher, mostly. But the point is, when I first went out for Little League, I didn't know how to do much. I didn't have a dad. My mom tried to throw a baseball with me, but she wasn't very good."

Danny nodded as if he understood.

Cassie wondered where this story was going.

"Anyway," Nash continued, "I was terrible at prac-tices, especially with batting. There were two older boys who kept making fun of me."

"What did you do?" Danny was listening intently now.

"I would have liked to have clocked them," Nash con-fessed. "But I got to know a police officer who often came to the school to talk with the kids. He told me the only way I could show up those boys was to get better. He offered to spend one night a week practic-ing with me."

"Did it work?" Danny wanted to know.

"It did. I soon started hitting balls instead of striking out, and my pitching arm got quite good. I guess what I'm trying to say is that fighting doesn't get the job done because nothing is resolved. There's always a way to settle a dispute without violence."

Cassie imagined Nash's story explained why he'd become a cop. But as a cop, he'd seen violence and that was why he had this philosophy.

Danny seemed to think about what Nash had said. "There's this one boy in art class who always makes fun of my drawings. I got really tired of it and pushed him. Then he hit me, and I hit him." He touched the bandage on his head.

"What are you going to do when you go back to school and have art class again?" Nash prodded.

"I don't want to go back to school. I want to drop art."

Now Cassie sat forward, too. "Danny, how would you feel if you could never paint again?"

"Terrible, but if people are just going to make fun of it…"

"Art is one of those things that you can't predict how people will react to," Cassie told him. "Look at me. I submitted my work for the arts festival and got turned down. Yes, it made me feel bad but I still want to paint, even if nobody else sees it. It helps me feel better."

"Painting and drawing help me feel better, too," Danny mumbled.

"Then why would you want to give it up?" Nash asked. "Because some dolt is jealous and knows you're better than he is?"

Danny's expression said that thought had never crossed his mind. "You really think that's the reason he picks on me?"

"I don't know for sure," Nash answered. "Your teacher might be able to shed light on that. I'm sure she's going to want a conference with your parents."

Danny's face fell.

"There *is* something else you could consider," Nash added. "Karate."

"I've only seen it in movies."

"Movies glamorize it a bit," Nash responded. "But there are maneuvers you can learn in karate that can help you deal with someone like a bully without actually hurting him."

"Really?" Danny asked.

Nash just nodded.

Suddenly the front door flew open and Danny's mom rushed in followed by a man Cassie had never met.

Dorie took one look at her son, saw the bandage on his head and hugged him. "Are you all right?"

"I'm fine, Mom, really I am," Danny assured her.

The man who had come in behind Dorie was frowning. "I'm Paul Lindstrom, Danny's father." He looked directly at Cassie. "I suppose you're the one who picked him up?"

Cassie squared her shoulders, not knowing exactly why. "I am."

"I'll be complaining to the school. You're a perfect stranger. I've never even met you before. What right do you have to pick up my son?"

"Paul, don't talk to Cassie that way," Dorie protested. "I put her name down as an emergency contact." She looked at Cassie apologetically. "I told him to meet me here if he wanted to be included in this discussion."

"Of course I'm going to be included in this discussion," Paul Lindstrom blustered. "My son was involved in a fight and got hurt."

"From what I understand, Mr. Lindstrom," Cassie said politely, "the other boy was hurt, too. He has a black eye."

Paul went to Danny and clapped him on the back. "Good going there. I didn't know you had it in you."

Cassie could have socked him, no matter what Nash said about nonviolence. Or maybe she just needed a few karate moves aimed at the right part of Danny's dad's body.

To Cassie's surprise, Danny stepped forward and faced his father. "Nash told me I don't need to hurt anyone. He said when words don't work, then karate moves might. I'd like to take karate along with art lessons."

"From what I understand, it's the art lessons that caused this whole problem. Somebody didn't like what you drew," his father reminded him.

"They were making fun of what I drew," Danny said, his eyes on his sneakers now.

"And what was that?" his father asked.

"A totem pole. They're real art objects, Dad. I saw a few of them online. But the boy I fought with said the Native Americans aren't real Americans and I said they were."

So this was about more than a drawing, Cassie thought. It always seemed to be.

Danny's father appeared not to know what to say to that. He cleared his throat, then asked, "And who's this Nash person you're talking about?"

Nash had been quiet up till now, just sitting back and observing. Since he'd been brought into the discussion, he stood and extended his hand to Danny's father. "I'm

Nash Tremont, a detective from Biloxi. I just happen to be staying here at the bed-and-breakfast. Danny and I have talked about his drawings before. He's very good. I imagine you're proud of him."

Cassie almost smiled. That certainly put Danny's father on the spot.

He blustered a bit and then declared, "Art lessons aren't going to lead him toward a career. He needs to find a hobby that will benefit his future."

"I won an art competition, and selling paintings enabled me to buy this bed-and-breakfast," Cassie told him proudly. "Danny could use his art in a million ways. It's up to him to find the best fit, or a counselor who understands his talents." She motioned toward the table at the side of the room. "Help yourself to a coffee and cookies. I want to show you something. I'll be right back."

She knew Nash could probably handle the conversation in the time it would take to pull Danny's folder out of her file cabinet. After she went to her room and did just that, she brought it back to the guest area. Paul was sitting on the sofa, munching on one of her cookies.

She sat next to him and handed him the folder. "Why don't you take a look at these? They're all pictures Danny has drawn. He's very talented."

After Paul paged through the folder, he sent a look to Nash that told Cassie he realized his son listened to him because he respected him.

"These are good," he confirmed. "He understands depth perception and shadowing. He's young for that."

"Since you understand that, maybe you had some art training?"

"I did as an undergraduate. I enjoyed it, but I realized

it really didn't fit into my curriculum since I wanted to become a lawyer."

"Maybe I like to draw because you did," Danny said, embracing Cassie's thoughts exactly.

"I suppose that's possible," Paul agreed. He rubbed his hand over his jaw. "I'm a corporate lawyer. I'm away on business so much that maybe I don't know what my son needs."

Dorie said in a soft voice, "If we talk to the principal together, maybe we'll get a better idea."

Danny's father nodded. "And we can talk about karate lessons if you're truly interested," he told his son.

"I am," Danny assured him.

Fifteen minutes later, the family left. After the door closed behind them, Nash asked, "Do you think they'll work it out?"

"Do you mean, will Danny's dad support his art? I don't know. I'd like to think people can change."

"They rarely do," Nash said, as if he knew that all too well.

"If Danny's dad can become interested in his son's art or even his karate training, then they'll have a common interest. That might be the first step to better communication."

"You *are* an optimist, aren't you?"

"I try to be. Is there a point to being negative instead of positive?"

Nash seemed to think about that. "Sometimes I'm flooded with the negative and I forget there's a positive. I'd like to think life can turn out well at the end, but when you're dealing with criminals and their habits, that's rarely true."

"Then we're back to whether anyone can change

or not. You know, you were really good with Danny. Maybe you should think about working with kids."

"When I was a beat cop, I did enjoy going to schools to talk about safety and the pitfalls of taking drugs."

"You talked to all ages of children?"

"Sure did, from bicycle safety with the first and second graders, up to the danger of drugs with the high school kids."

Cassie couldn't help herself from asking, "Do you want your own kids some day?"

"I thought about it when I believed I'd be engaged to Sara, but I guess I just put any thoughts about kids on hold since then. Do *you* want children?"

"I'd love to have children. But I'd have to meet the right man."

"Yes, I guess you would," Nash agreed, his gaze locking to hers.

When Cassie's cell phone dinged, the sound seemed to startle them both.

Nash asked, "Since no guests signed up for dinner tonight, are you interested in pancakes and bacon? I'm an expert chef at those."

Going to the counter to pick up her phone, Cassie nodded. "Pancakes would be great. After I get this, I'll help you."

She didn't recognize the number the caller ID showed—Senft Art Gallery. Why would an art gallery be calling her?

"Hello? This is Cassie Calloway at the Bluebonnet Bed-and-Breakfast."

"Miss Calloway, this is Mark Senft from the Senft Gallery. I'll get right to the point. I'd like to see your portfolio and meet you in person. Would that be possible tomorrow at 11 a.m.? That meeting would be in my office in Round Rock."

"How did you hear about my work?" she asked.

"I received an email with photo files from your agent."

"My agent," she repeated.

"Yes, Nash Tremont."

"I see," she said slowly, turning her gaze on Nash. "I forgot he was sending that out this week."

"So you've queried other galleries?"

"Yes," she said, not knowing whether that was true or not. She'd have to ask Nash.

"Have you made other appointments?" Senft asked.

"Not yet."

"Well, good. Can you meet with me tomorrow?"

"Yes, I can. Eleven, you say? Can you give me your address again?"

He did.

"I'll see you tomorrow at eleven."

After the requisite goodbyes, Cassie laid her cell phone on the counter and approached Nash. He'd just taken a frying pan from a lower cupboard.

"What did you do?" she asked.

"I was hoping I was doing something nice for you. Did it work out?"

"I don't know yet. I'm meeting Mr. Senft tomorrow. Did you query other galleries?"

"Yes, I did. About nine of them. So you might be getting other phone calls."

"Nash, you're wonderful." She couldn't help but throw her arms around his neck. After she did, they studied each other for a very long moment. In the next heartbeat, he was bending his head, holding her tight, kissing her with a fervor that made her want him in an elemental way.

As Cassie drowned in his kiss, she realized he kissed in layers—soft and coaxing first, then with some sweet taunting, and finally with a passion that not only took her breath away but shooed common sense into a corner of her mind where it wasn't yelling at her. But she knew better than to get involved with him. His body was hard and muscled and strong. With him holding her this tightly, she could tell. His chest was broad, his stomach was taut, his thighs as they pressed against her legs were solidly immovable.

This time, with this kiss, he didn't break away quickly and neither did she. It was as if they reveled in what they were doing. While his right hand held her close, his left brushed her back creating delicious shivers along her spine. Cassie wished the kiss could go on forever.

"You taste as delicious as your cinnamon rolls," he whispered on an indrawn breath. Then he was kissing her again.

She should have backed away. She should have told him to stop. But stopping didn't seem to be in her vocabulary at that moment. And the moment stretched and stretched and stretched. This was closer than she'd been to a man in years. And not just physically. She felt close to Nash emotionally. His kisses stirred up feelings and sensations that she'd long forgotten. She was totally caught up in Nash, not just the kiss. She reveled in the scent of him, in his male pheromones that seemed to unite with her female ones. Her hand caressed his neck as she pushed tighter against him. She heard the growl in his throat. Because he was aroused? Because he needed a woman? Because he needed *her*. She should be afraid of this much excitement…this much hunger. She should be afraid of making a fool of herself over a man who was going to leave. But she couldn't stop herself.

It was Nash who broke away. His eyes were stormy as he looked down at her and asked, "Was that kiss because I did a favor for you?"

It took her a minute to gather her thoughts and to remember where she was. It was difficult because she was still tingling from every sensation she'd felt while he kissed her.

"Of course not," she said. "Why would you think that?"

"Because you didn't pull away. I don't need thanks for what I did."

Feeling a little indignant and misunderstood, she took a step back. "If I wanted to thank you, I'd bake you more cinnamon rolls or chocolate chip cookies. Why did you kiss me?"

"Because that's all I've been thinking about since our last kiss."

She blinked at him. "Nash, this is crazy."

"Crazy it might be, but it's happening."

"What exactly is happening?"

He ran his hand through his hair. "I wish I knew. I just know I like being around you. I definitely like kissing you."

"Do you often kiss women when you go to a strange town?"

"No," Nash said, shaking his head. "Why would you think that after I told you about Sara?"

"Maybe *because* of Sara. Maybe you don't want any

attachment. Maybe kissing and sleeping with a woman is all you need. Or else you've convinced yourself that's all you need."

"So now you've turned into a psychologist?"

"No. I've turned into a woman who doesn't want to get hurt. You haven't answered my question."

"I shouldn't have to. But just for the sake of clarity, no, I don't sleep around, whether I'm at home or on the road. That's not me. I've dated since I've lived in Biloxi, but nothing ever came of it. So I just stopped."

"We're not exactly dating," she reminded him.

"Sure, we are. We went to lunch. We went to the zoo."

If this weren't so serious, she'd laugh. But it was serious because that kiss had made her realize she was in love with Nash Tremont, or fully on the way to it. Yet she couldn't really tell where he stood in all this.

"Tell me something, Nash. What if you find the information you're looking for? What if your month is up and you drive back to Biloxi? What if you think about kissing me while you're there? What happens next?"

"You're asking about a future I don't have a road map for. I can't tell you what's going to happen in a week or two or three. I don't have a crystal ball. Do you?"

His comment made her sound as if she was being totally illogical and completely unreasonable. But she wasn't. She always had to have a plan. Ever since she was a kid, when there was little food in the cupboard, there was a neighbor she could clean for, make some money and buy groceries. When her mother didn't show up at school for a conference, or anything else that was important to Cassie, she had a whole line of excuses in her mind why her mother couldn't be there. One or another would roll off her tongue as if it were the truth. If her mother didn't come home at night, Cassie would visit a friend, and those friends would ask her to stay over and spend the night. She wouldn't have to be in the apartment alone. But she couldn't say any of this to Nash.

Well, maybe she could say a little. "I had a lot of uncertainty in my life as a child, Nash. As I grew up, I wanted my life planned. I have part-time jobs so if I don't have enough guests in a month, I can still pay my mortgage. I like to know what meal I'm cooking tomorrow so I have the ingredients for it. I ask my guests if they have any allergies so I don't step into a crisis inadvertently. That's just me. So if I begin caring for you and you just leave, that's not okay for me."

"Cassie…" He reached out a hand to her, but she stepped back.

"I appreciate what you did for me, I really do. Right now I'm going to go up to the attic and pick out a few paintings to take along with me to my appointment tomorrow."

"Take the new one," he said.

"The new one isn't finished."

"That doesn't matter. It shows your talent."

"I'll think about it. You were going to make yourself pancakes. Go ahead and do that. The kitchen's yours. And tomorrow when I get back, I'll bake you cinnamon rolls as a real thank-you."

This time *she* was the one who left the room. *She* was the one who climbed the stairs. *She* was the one who turned her back on heartache.

Chapter Eleven

Cassie was so excited when she returned from her appointment in Round Rock the following day. She parked her car in the gravel area behind the B&B, a wide smile still on her face. She'd been wearing it the whole way back from Round Rock. She was going to have an art show sometime this summer! Mr. Senft was going to call her with the date next week.

She wanted to tell Nash. She wanted to thank him again. But then she remembered how they'd left things last night. She hadn't seen him this morning. He hadn't even stopped for his usual mug of coffee. Either he'd left early or he'd been doing research in his room. She really had no right to know, either way. That made her sad.

She opened the back door of her car and pulled out the three paintings she'd taken along to show Mr. Senft.

She'd been up half the night finishing the angel, but she, of course, couldn't take that one along because it was still wet. She had taken a picture of it, though, with her phone. Nash might have been right about that, too. That was the painting that might have decided the gallery owner in her favor.

She was carrying the paintings up the back walk when she spotted Renata tending to the herb garden in her backyard. It was a raised bin so she didn't have to stoop over so far to reach it.

Renata waved to her. "Where have you been?" her neighbor asked her.

"Let me set these paintings inside the porch, then I'll come over and tell you." Cassie ran up the steps, deposited the paintings inside and then went back to Renata's yard. The smile was back on her face as she thought about her good news.

"You look happy," Renata said.

"I am *so* happy. My paintings are going to be shown in a gallery this summer."

"Which gallery would that be?"

"Mr. Senft, from Round Rock, has galleries in Austin, San Antonio and Dallas. He thinks he wants to set me up in the San Antonio gallery. He's going to let me know next week about that and a date."

Renata threw her arms around Cassie, making tears spring to Cassie's eyes. Her neighbor had become a mother figure in her life when she'd sorely needed one. "That's wonderful news, honey. I guess you took paintings along to show this Mr. Senft?"

"I did, along with a picture or two. Nash had already sent him photos of my work with a letter."

Renata leaned back. "Nash did?"

"Yes. He said he wanted to do something nice for me."

"That man cares about you. I can see it in his eyes."

Caring was one thing. Attraction was another. Maybe Renata had mistaken one for the other.

When Cassie didn't respond, Renata said, "You don't believe me, do you?"

"I like Nash, and I think he likes me. But we haven't known each other very long, and he's going to be leaving in another week or so."

Renata studied her. "Would you like him to stay?"

"He can't do that. He has a job in Biloxi."

"I see," Renata said with a twinkle in her eye. "You know, I have heard of these things called airplanes that fly back and forth, and cars that make trips comfortable."

Cassie laughed. "I understand. You get around."

"I not only get around, I'm old enough to have experience of the heart. My Luis and I, well, it was love at first sight."

"Where did you meet?"

"At the wedding of a friend. He knew the groom, and I knew the bride. We began talking over dinner, we danced, and that was it. We were married for forty-five years."

"I can't even imagine," Cassie said.

"When you're in love, when you have a life together, time passes by much too quickly. I only wish we'd had children. We took in two foster children."

"Where are they now?"

"The little girl, Olivia, was reunited with her mother after two years with us. Her mother got clean from drugs and every once in a while, I get a letter from her. Olivia has her own family now and lives in Kansas."

"And the other child?"

"Billy was a wanderer. He came to us when he was sixteen because he had nowhere else to go. He was all defiance and rebellion at first, but then Luis and he found some common ground. They both liked to fish. Billy stayed with us until he earned enough to buy his own car, and then he was gone. The last time I heard from him, he was running one of those shops along the beach in Venice, California. He usually calls me on Christmas."

Cassie imagined there was so much more about Renata she didn't know, but she did know one thing. Her birthday was tomorrow and Cassie was throwing a party. Renata deserved some caring, and Cassie wanted to make her feel special.

Renata patted Cassie's arm. "Someday you'll marry and have children, and then you'll have wonderful memories like I do." Cassie didn't know if that would ever be true, but she could hope.

Renata turned back to her herb bin. "Do you need any fresh herbs for your meals today?"

Cassie thought about the roast she was going to put in the oven. Three guests were staying for dinner tonight. Nash hadn't signed up, and she hadn't spoken to him so she didn't know if he'd be around. "I could use marjoram and thyme. I want to make a rub for the roast. Maybe parsley, too. I might make parsley buttered potatoes."

Renata had her snippers right at the bin. She said, "I'll clip some for you."

"Would you like some roast beef and potatoes and green beans tonight? I'll have plenty."

"Cassie, you're too good to me."

"Not possible."

"Hold out your hands," Renata said.

Cassie did as she was told.

Renata placed the stems of marjoram and thyme in Cassie's hands, then laid longer stems of parsley across those. "Don't drop them," she warned.

"I won't. I'll bring your meal over as soon as I serve my guests."

Renata's eyes grew suspiciously moist. She gave Cassie a hug. When Cassie left the protection of the older woman's arms to head for her own house, she missed them. She missed her mother, too, the mother she'd really never had.

Cassie went to bed that night with the scent of cinnamon rolls still pervading the bed-and-breakfast. She'd made them for Nash as a thank-you, and it was a point she wanted to emphasize. She'd left them on the desk wrapped in foil with Nash's name affixed to the package. Before she'd turned in tonight, they'd been gone, so she assumed he'd gotten them.

She tried not to think of Nash but rather concentrated on the show she was going to have this summer. She had paintings in her head that her fingers were itching to paint onto canvas. She thought about painting before bed, but it seemed more important to get a good night's sleep and start fresh in the morning. When she turned off the light, she expected to do just that.

However, she tossed and turned for about an hour, finally falling into a restless sleep. A dream began pleasantly enough. She was on a street lined with vibrant colored flowers and oil paintings in every style. But as she walked up the street, she suddenly felt as if someone were following her. She glanced over her shoulder but could only spot a shadow. As she walked faster, the shadow came after her faster.

She began jogging and the shadow seemed to jog, too. Next, she was running full out. The flowers disappeared. The paintings disappeared. Dilapidated row houses lined both sides of the street. She was streaking by them so fast she didn't know if she might have lived in one of them. Faster and faster she ran. There were no sidewalks here but she was running along the yellow line in the middle of the road.

Suddenly a car was speeding toward her but it wasn't on *its* side of the road. It was in the middle. It began weaving back and forth in wide swerves. She knew she should run back the way she'd come or run over to the side. But it was as if her feet were entrenched on that yellow line in the middle of the road. The car kept coming closer and her mother was driving. The car was going to hit her.

She was calling her mother's name. Screaming. Out of nowhere somebody grabbed her and pulled her out of the way just as the car reached her.

She woke up still screaming. Someone was rocking her in his arms, stroking her hair, murmuring, "Shush. You're all right."

She realized her hair was matted to her head. She was shaking, and she was in Nash's arms.

He held her protectively, stroking her cheek, brushing her hair out of her eyes. "You're fine," he said.

"You're safe." His strong baritone commanded her to believe it.

What she couldn't believe was that the dream had seemed so real. She grabbed onto Nash, still feeling a bit crazed. "A car was coming toward me. My—" She stopped. "It was going to hit me."

Nash was studying her, looking genuinely concerned. "Do you want to tell me what else was in the dream?"

She didn't want to talk about it. If she did, she could let something slip. She was sure the dream had something to do with her childhood and the fact that her mother was now in prison. But she couldn't say any of that to Nash.

She sat up straighter. "I'll be okay. Really, I will."

It was apparent that Nash didn't believe her. He just sat there holding her, and she let him because the strength of his arms felt so good around her.

"Dreams can be a way your mind settles problems. They bring fears to the surface so you can deal with them."

"You've had dream therapy?" she tried to joke.

"No, but I have had some training in PTSD, and a bit of psychology." Nash was still rocking her gently.

Cassie didn't want to delve into the psychology of her dream. She didn't want to talk about it at all. "Did you eat the cinnamon rolls?" she asked, hoping he'd drop the subject.

"I ate two and I have one left."

"You don't have to save it. I have some left for breakfast if you want them then."

"I'll keep that in mind."

The longer he held her, the more she could feel heat building between them. He was wearing a light T-shirt and soft lounge pants. She could not only see the muscles under his shirt, but she could feel them. She was so tired of fighting the attraction between them. In some ways, the dream had made her aware of how short life was. Maybe it was time she lived it instead of watching it pass her by.

She looked up at Nash, knowing what she felt was apparent in her eyes. She didn't know how to hide that kind of feeling. She didn't know how to hide the fact that she was falling in love with him.

"I want to kiss you, Cassie. In fact, I want to do more than kiss you. But I feel you're vulnerable right now, and I don't want to take advantage of you."

Nothing else Nash said could have made him more endearing to her. He was still trying to protect her, setting his needs aside.

"I'm not vulnerable. Since you've been here, a wall or two has fallen down. Why shouldn't I enjoy myself? Why shouldn't I enjoy *you*? It's silly to pretend we don't want each other when we do."

"You make it sound so reasonable." He ran his thumb over her bottom lip. She trembled and this time it wasn't because of the dream.

Nash's hand was a bit rough as he cupped her face. She took it and felt it, running her fingers over a callus or two. "You've done hard work."

"I told you I worked construction. Back when I was in high school I helped to build houses. So at times, in between investigations, I help to build houses for organizations like Homes for Families. I don't want to forget all those skills I learned."

When she still fingered his palm, he closed his eyes for a moment. She kissed one of the calluses and he let out a groan. "Cassie." Her name was a warning that she didn't intend to heed. She kissed his palm again.

"You shouldn't," he growled.

"Why not?"

"Because I might end up in this bed with you."

His words were so arousing she wasn't sure what to do next. But as she kept her gaze locked to his, his hands slid along her collarbone. She loved the feel of his skin on hers. Her heart raced and her stomach felt as if it were somersaulting. She didn't want to reach for him because she felt she'd been forward enough. What if he didn't want her? What if he didn't want to make love with her?

But she needn't have worried. He bent his head and murmured, "I came down to the kitchen for a glass of milk to have with that cinnamon roll, but I heard you screaming even through your door. It wasn't locked. Why don't you keep it locked?"

"Usually I do, but tonight I was distracted."

He bent his head closer to hers. "I'm distracted by *you*, morning, noon and night. But especially at night."

So he *did* want her. At first, she thought she was hearing the ticking of her clock on her bedside stand, but then she realized she was hearing her heart pounding and maybe his. When his kiss came, it drew her out of herself and into him. Before his kisses had seemed to have finesse. This one didn't. This one was abject hunger, on his part and on hers. She welcomed his tongue into her mouth. She couldn't seem to get close enough to him. Desire mixed with the exquisite feeling of being wanted. She kissed him back as if he didn't live in Biloxi, as if he weren't going to leave, as if he weren't involved in an investigation that could change his life in so many ways. She almost felt dizzy with the need he created in her.

He caressed her, his hands blazing a trail of heat through her nightgown, making her crazy with need. He dropped kisses onto her neck, nuzzled her nose and whispered, "Maybe we should take off your nightgown."

"It's about time you suggested it."

He laughed and took hold of the hem. It was up and over her head and on the floor in no time. "I don't know why women wear nightgowns," he said. "You should just go to bed nude."

"Do you?" she returned, amused.

"I do," he assured her.

She knew she'd keep with her the picture of Nash in his bed naked for all time. But soon she'd have an even better picture to remember. She pulled the drawstring at his waist.

"Tit for tat?" he asked.

"Something like that, unless you want to keep your clothes on."

"Not a chance," he said gruffly, proceeding to rid himself of his clothes.

Nash kissed her with renewed passion, but then suddenly broke away. "I hate to take the romance out of this, but I have to ask. Do you have any condoms?"

As her brain and her body settled from his kiss, the question suddenly resonated. She shook her head slowly back and forth. "No."

Nash's face fell, and his brows drew together. He seemed to move away from her a little. Before he could, she took hold of his hand and interlaced her fingers with his. "I'm on the pill, Nash." She knew he was going to wonder why when she said she didn't date. So she explained, "My doctor put me on it to help with my periods. I was having bad cramps." She saw the look on his face that said he wasn't used to discussing this, and she almost laughed. But she didn't. "I hope that doesn't come under the category of too much information, but I'm not going to get pregnant if that's what you're worried about."

He took her into his arms again. "Nothing's too much information when it's about *you*."

She didn't know if a man had ever said something so nice to her. She felt tears burning in her eyes.

As they lay there, skin against skin in her single bed, she could detect the scent of soap on Nash. He must have gotten a shower before he'd gone to bed. "You smell good," she said, nuzzling his chest.

"So do you," he murmured as he nipped at her shoulder. "You always seem to smell like cinnamon and vanilla."

"I don't know if that's good or bad," she said with a laugh.

"It's good, very good." Then Nash began to tell her in actions rather than in words.

His lips and tongue explored her all over with excruciating, sensual fervor. Cassie never expected she'd be capable of the passion that Nash drew from her. His every kiss and touch was exciting and brand-new. It all seemed so natural—his thumb teasing her nipple, his lips kissing her navel, his hands gently separating her thighs. In some ways Cassie wanted to prolong each kiss and each caress. In other ways, she wanted to hurry and find the satisfaction she knew Nash could give her.

She enjoyed exploring his male body—the definition, the strength, the tautness that she knew was due to tension because he was holding back. His next kiss was a claiming kiss, and she realized what it meant. They were both ready. As he rose above her, she gazed into his eyes, just trying to see the present because they might not have a future. Sadness about that didn't have a chance to take hold.

Nash urged her to raise her legs and she did. She wrapped them around his waist as he entered her slowly, teasing her with a fulfillment that they both wanted. Cassie felt the sensual excitement and pleasure that had eluded her all of her adult life as Nash thrust into her, withdrew and then thrust again. She knew with absolute certainty that tonight she was losing her heart to him completely. When her climax engulfed her, his engulfed him. Together they shouted each other's names. Together they found supreme pleasure. Not long after, Cassie fell asleep in Nash's arms, totally content to be exactly where she was.

Cassie awakened at daylight as she usually did. She could see the sunrise through the curtains at her window. Everything about last night came back, every memory, every pleasure, but she wasn't sure how to deal with it. She glanced over her shoulder at Nash, but didn't want to wake him. She'd simply slip out of bed, go to the kitchen and prepare a casserole for breakfast.

But as she moved only a few inches, Nash snagged her around her waist with his arm. "Going somewhere?" he asked into her ear.

She swallowed hard. "I was going to get breakfast ready."

He rubbed his chin against her shoulder. "Isn't it too early for breakfast?"

"Not if the egg has to soak into the bread, and I have to make bacon to top it with, and—" She was rambling but Nash stopped her.

"I get that you're rattled. I am, too. But don't you think we should talk about it?"

"Is there anything to talk about?"

"I guess not if you don't think there is."

He sounded…disappointed. She turned around to face him. "Last night was wonderful."

"Then why are you running off? Do you regret it?"

"I don't have any regrets," she assured him. She had no regrets because she knew she was already in love with Nash. But he was going to be leaving town soon. Could she coax him to stay?

"Then what's wrong?" he asked.

"Because you're leaving, this…" she motioned to the two of them in the bed. "Whatever this is has an expiration date."

"Only if we want it to," he said.

She was reminded of Renata's advice that there were planes and cars that could help a long-distance relationship.

However, distance wasn't the real problem for Cassie. She maybe could fly back and forth or drive back and forth to Biloxi, or maybe he could. No, the real problem was the truth that reared its ugly head between them. If they continued whatever was building between them, she'd have to tell him that her mother was in prison. Once she did that, he'd leave anyway. He had to. She knew what he thought about law and order. She knew he believed right and wrong was cut-and-dried, black-

and-white. To Cassie, her mom being in prison was all kinds of shades of gray.

"I really do have to start breakfast," she reminded him. "Can we talk again later?" That would give her time to think about it more.

He frowned. "We can talk later." He sat up on the edge of the bed, grabbed his pants and started putting them on.

"I'm throwing a birthday party for Renata tonight," she told him as she lay there. "A few neighbors are coming. I just want to make her feel special. I have a birthday cake to bake, too. Will you be around this evening?" She couldn't keep the hopefulness from her voice.

He turned to her and she saw that his frown had disappeared. "I wouldn't want to be anywhere else. What can I get her?"

"I got her a velvet throw for her sofa, though she insists she doesn't need anything. If you really want to get her something—"

"Tell me what you have in mind."

"I know she likes baskets. She has one that she uses to carry in vegetables from her garden. But hers is practically coming apart."

"All right. I passed one of those home stores. They should have baskets, shouldn't they?"

"They should."

"And I could fill it with things she needs—dish detergent, tissues, plastic wrap, that kind of thing."

"That's a wonderful idea!"

Cassie slipped her nightgown over her head and stood up. "So we'll talk tonight after the party?"

Rising to his feet, Nash plucked his shirt from the

floor. "We will." Then he gave her a kiss that told her he remembered everything about last night, too.

As he left her room, Cassie wondered if she'd have the courage tonight to tell him about her mother.

Chapter Twelve

Nash couldn't stop thinking about last night while he showered. Visions of making love to Cassie filled his mind and his heart. He hadn't felt anything near to this with Sara. What did that tell him?

That he was seeing something in Cassie that wasn't there? That he had healed from his relationship with Sara? That enough time had passed and romance now seemed a possibility?

Maybe all of the above.

He took his time dressing because today he simply didn't think he could keep his mind on research, records and the Robinson family.

He still had one of the cinnamon rolls Cassie had left him last night. Perfect. He took a bottle of water from the six-pack he'd brought to his room. Other than picking up Renata's present, he needed to hole up in here today and shut out the rest of the world. Maybe then he'd get some clarity on all of it.

Because after Mrs. Garcia's party, he and Cassie were going to have a talk. The problem was he had no idea what he was going to say.

Opening the bottle of water, he took a few swigs and settled at his desk. There he opened the foil that he'd re-wrapped around the lone cinnamon roll. Cassie's thank-you present. He sighed. In some ways, she was a tough nut to crack. He still didn't know that much about her, other than the fact that she came from Bryan. He wondered if the Austin library would have yearbooks from Bryan. Maybe he could learn something more about her from the yearbook.

He'd finished the last of the cinnamon roll and wiped his hands on a napkin when his cell phone buzzed.

It was early. Who could be calling him? Had his supervisor somehow learned what he was up to?

Only one way to find out. But when he checked the screen, he saw the caller had a blocked number. In the past he'd worked with confidential informants who had blocked numbers and burner phones. Back then it hadn't been that unusual. But now...

Needing a distraction, he decided to answer. "Tremont here."

"I understand you're looking for information on the Robinson family."

Nash didn't recognize the voice. And just who could know he was looking for information? He immediately distrusted whoever was calling. "What makes you think that?"

"I have connections," the male voice said. "But if you want the info I have, you have to meet with me."

"I suppose you have a meeting place picked out?"

"No, I don't. That's up to you."

That took Nash aback. Usually when someone like this anonymous source wanted to meet, they decided where the meeting was held.

Was he even going to this meeting? He was going nowhere fast enough on his own. Maybe this was the source he needed.

It was too early to meet at a bar, but Nash didn't want this meeting to wait. "There's a restaurant that serves great pancakes and strong coffee. How about meeting me at Dusty's Diner in an hour." He rattled off the address.

"That doesn't give me much time," the man said.

"Why do you need time if you're just going to give me information?"

"All right. I'll meet you in an hour at Dusty's Diner. I know what you look like."

"I'll be carrying," Nash said. His service weapon was locked in the glove compartment of his SUV, but maybe this was the time to take it out. After all, he knew many people in Austin had concealed handgun permits.

"Not necessary," the man on the other end of the line protested.

"We'll see about that. An hour. Don't be late." Nash ended the call.

He didn't know if he was doing the smart thing or a foolish thing, but he might as well get to Dusty's early and have eggs and coffee before his informant met him. He might not have the stomach for it afterward.

An hour later Nash had eaten eggs, toast and drunk two cups of coffee when a man in a suit walked through the door. Nash sat perfectly still in the rear booth. This guy looked out of place in the diner. Could he actually be Nash's informant? Nash felt the weight of his gun under his jacket. He knew from experience that you could never just go by looks.

The stranger walked toward him. The thing was, he looked familiar. Nash had checked out so many photos of the Fortunes and the Robinsons that he supposed he could have seen this man's picture somewhere.

The man stood at Nash's table and just stared at him. Then he extended his hand. "I'm Ben Fortune Robinson."

That surprised Nash.

The man didn't sit. He stood beside the table and said, "My family has connections all over Austin. There's no way you could inquire too deeply into the Robinsons without us finding out. Why didn't you just call one of us and meet with the family in person if you have questions? It would have been so much easier and it's what we've wanted all along."

"I'm not sure I want it easy," Nash said. "I didn't expect anything about this to be easy. The kind of information I'm looking for isn't the kind the family would want to give me." He kept a hard edge to his tone so Ben Robinson knew he was serious.

Ben turned to look out the window and motioned to someone, putting Nash on guard.

"Calling in reinforcements?" Nash asked.

"I don't need reinforcements, but *you* might."

At first Nash felt outnumbered when a man in a charcoal suit came through the diner's glass door, but he knew he could take both men down if he had to.

As the other stranger approached, Nash's glare must have been strong enough and hard enough that both of them understood what Nash was thinking. They both raised their hands at the same time and opened their suit jackets so Nash could see they had no weapons.

The newcomer extended his hand to Nash. "I'm Keaton Whitfield, one of Gerald Robinson's illegitimate children," he said in a slight English accent. "For some reason, this feels like a Grade B movie."

Nash relaxed a bit, studying the two men as they sat in the booth across from him.

The waitress came over, and Ben and Keaton ordered coffee. She brought it and then left again.

Ben looked Nash in the eye. "We know what you must think about Gerald Robinson leaving your mom high and dry."

So they had done their homework, Nash thought. Still he kept silent, letting them fill it.

"We're not bad people, no matter what you've heard about Gerald," Keaton added.

"Does Gerald know I'm in town?" Nash asked.

Ben shook his head. "No. While you were going about your investigation incognito, you obviously wanted to keep your distance. We didn't want to blind-side you, but we want you to consider something. We *are* your half brothers."

Nash sighed. Of course they'd play *that* card. "You think that means anything?" he asked.

Ben frowned. "It could. What exactly do you want to know?"

"First of all, I want to keep my identity under wraps," Nash insisted.

"You don't want anyone to know you're a Fortune?" Keaton surmised.

"I'm *not* a Fortune," Nash protested adamantly. "I'm a Tremont."

Ben and Keaton exchanged a look. "We understand where you're coming from," Keaton said. "We've been there."

During the next fifteen minutes, Nash tried to determine if Ben and Keaton knew he was investigating Charlotte Robinson. They didn't seem to. So his secret was safe, though he didn't know for how long. At any time, these two men could tell Gerald he was in town, not to mention Charlotte. Charlotte was the Robinson he wanted to nail.

After about fifteen minutes of Nash asking questions, and Ben and Keaton answering, he realized these two men actually seemed like good guys. Could he deny getting to know his half brothers? Especially if they were on the up-and-up?

Nash addressed Keaton. "Lucie Fortune Chesterfield Parker connected you with Ben, didn't she? I saw that somewhere."

"She did," Keaton answered easily. "Lucie's a doll. We just happened to know each other in England. I designed a house for one of her mother's friends and Lucie and I ran into each other at a few parties. When Ben asked for an introduction to me, she didn't hesitate. She's like that."

Nash remembered reading that Ben Fortune Robinson had married a woman named Ella Thomas. He didn't know much about Keaton Whitfield.

Ben took a business card from the inside pocket of his suit jacket and passed it over to Nash. "I have the feeling you haven't asked us the questions you really want to ask. You're looking for something and we might be able to help you."

Keaton passed his card to Nash, too. "You can call either one of us at any time. We *do* want to help. We are related and the truth is, a detective in the family wouldn't be a bad thing." Keaton's eyes actually had some amusement in them.

Nash wished he could be amused. "I'll keep that in mind," he said, picking up the cards and inserting them into his jacket pocket.

Keaton laid some bills on the table. "Call us. If Gerald does happen to find out you're in town—and that won't happen through us—we'll let you know."

"I'm only going to be in town another week or so."

Ben said, "We're glad we met you. We hope you're glad you met us."

At that, both men exited the booth and left the restaurant.

Nash watched them go, not sure what to do next.

Cassie was putting the final touches of decorations on Renata's cake when Nash returned to the bed-and-breakfast late morning. He looked agitated, she thought. After a slight nod her way, he went to the coffee urn and poured himself a mug.

She was studying his face when he looked up at her and shook his head. "I probably don't need more caffeine in addition to everything else," he said, putting down the mug.

Finishing off the cake, she put it into the refrigerator, then she joined Nash.

"Is something wrong?"

He looked pensive for a moment before he said, "It's complicated." His expression became closed.

So conversation wasn't what he wanted right now. She murmured, "Sorry for prying again," and started walking down the hall to her room. But she didn't even get halfway there.

Nash strode after her, caught her arm and stopped her. "Cassie, this doesn't have anything to do with you and me. It has to do with the Fortunes and the Robinsons."

She looked him straight in the eyes. "Do you want to talk about it?"

After studying her a good long time, he nodded. She motioned toward her bedroom. Why not? It wasn't as if the bed was going to tempt them any more than it had before.

After they sat on the love seat together, Nash took off his Stetson and laid it on a nearby table. Then he rubbed his hands down over his face.

"Nash, what happened?"

"I got an anonymous call this morning. A man said he had information on the Robinsons for me, or the Fortunes. However you want to look at it. He wouldn't give me his name and he set up a meeting. I picked the place. I waited at Dusty's Diner."

She knew the spot where breakfasts were cheap.

"It turns out the man was Ben Fortune Robinson. Then he introduced Keaton Whitfield, too. Both of them are my half brothers."

Cassie knew a small gasp escaped her. "How did that go?"

"Ben said he called anonymously because he didn't

think I'd meet him if I knew who he was. He's probably right." Nash related the main parts of their conversation.

Cassie summed it up. "So you met two of your half brothers but you didn't tell them why you're really here."

He must have sensed disapproval in her tone because he turned away from her, studied the wall and said tersely, "I don't owe them or Gerald Robinson anything. If my biological father's wife is a criminal, she deserves to be arrested and brought to trial. I can't take a chance in telling either Ben or Keaton the truth. They could reveal it to Gerald or Charlotte. Both could try to wipe away any evidence."

Easily seeing his point, Cassie said, "Nash, I'm not judging you."

He turned to look at her once more, and she hoped the only thing on her face was the caring she felt for him. He must have seen that because he took her hand and rubbed his thumb against hers. Even that slight touch made Cassie want to be held in his arms again. But as he said, this wasn't about them.

She squeezed his hand so he knew she was sympathetic to what he'd said. But then she explained what she was thinking. "I'm just wondering if you realize how many bridges you'll be burning in pursuing Charlotte. What if you change your mind in a little while and you want to get to know your dad?"

"I won't want that," Nash insisted.

"If that's true, then why do you seem so upset?"

It took Nash long moments to answer. "Maybe because it's possible that Ben and Keaton are just caught up in this whole thing like I am, only in a different way. Besides that, I'm just angry that I'm going to have to approach this case from a different angle now. It's quite possible that either Ben or Keaton have a PI on me to keep up with what I'm doing while I'm here."

"An investigator on the investigator," she murmured.

"I don't know if they would do that, but they don't know me any more than I know them."

"You liked them, didn't you?"

"If my judgment wasn't clouded by how personally involved I am in this, I'd say they both seemed like upright guys. Everything about their backgrounds points in that direction, too. Another time in another place, we might even have been friends."

"It's all right if you feel something toward your half brothers…even toward your father. Can't you realize that?"

He blew out a long breath. "The only thing I'm realizing right now, is how much I'm beginning to care for *you*."

At that admission, Cassie wrapped her arms around him and hugged him. But that hug soon became much more as Nash bent his head and kissed her. Whereas they'd been talking about the Robinsons and the Fortunes and Nash had declared his upset had nothing to do with him and Cassie, the silent conversation between them suddenly changed. No longer was this about the Fortunes and the Robinsons. The kiss was about her and Nash—and *only* her and Nash.

His lips were hot and she returned their fire. His tongue was rough and she returned his need. Somehow he released passion she never knew she possessed. Somehow he was making her dream beyond the present. He cupped her face while he kissed her and every moment of that was sensual, too.

He broke away to insinuate his fingers underneath

the hem of her top. "I dreamed of doing this again," he said.

Of doing this again, she repeated in her mind. What was *this*? Did that mean he was falling for her the same way she was falling for him? Did it mean they were about to give more than their bodies to each other, but their trust, too? Could she really do that?

Fortunately, his actions made her forget everything else. He was lifting her top up and over her head, and she cooperated because she'd dreamed of making love to him again. That was how *she* thought of it.

It wasn't long before she was naked before him. The odd thing was, she didn't feel self-conscious. She felt proud that he was looking at her as if she were one of those cinnamon rolls he liked so much. His eyes devoured her and her anticipation grew. For some reason, she realized she had to be his equal. She couldn't just stand by and be a passive participant. Not in this.

Reaching out, she took hold of his belt buckle and unfastened it. A look of surprise crossed his face.

He asked, "Do you want help?"

"I've got it," she said confidently.

"Yes, you do," he agreed, and she felt as if he'd just told her she was the most beautiful woman in the world.

All was quiet in the house. She didn't even hear the creak of a floorboard or the tinkling of water from a spigot.

"I want to tell you something," she said, as she unzipped his fly.

"Something important?" he asked, his voice obviously strained.

"I don't know if it's important to you, but it is important to me. I've never had an orgasm before last night."

His eyes came open. Gruffly he took her hands in his and said, "That's it. I'm taking off the rest of my clothes."

She couldn't help but smile. "I don't mind doing it for you."

"If you do it for me, we're not going to have a reason to get into that bed."

A few minutes later, he was naked, too, and they were both in bed, tight against each other. He pushed her hair away from her face and let his fingers linger in it. "You know, last night was the first I've been in a single bed since I was a kid."

"How does it feel?" she asked, reaching for his chest, running her fingers lightly over his nipple.

He groaned. "Right now I feel like I've landed in my idea of heaven."

He kissed the soft spot behind her ear, kissed the pulse point at her throat and slowly made his way to her breasts. He raised his head to see her reaction and smiled. "Your cheeks are pink."

"That's because I'm hot all over."

He bent his head again and murmured, "The nice thing about a single bed is that it keeps you close."

He was making her crazy with need. She wanted to do the same to him. Reaching between them, she stroked his thigh. "How close do you want to get?"

"This close," he said, rubbing against her so she knew exactly how much he wanted her.

They kissed as if they couldn't get enough of each other. Maybe because they knew they had a time limit, maybe because the clock was ticking until the day he left for Biloxi. As she touched him more intimately, he kissed her harder. Suddenly Nash pulled her on top of him. She straddled his legs and looked down at him gazing up at her.

He said, "We'll have a little more freedom this way."

Freedom was a funny word. She felt free to be sensual with Nash, sexual in a way she hadn't been with anyone else ever before. Yet she didn't feel the freedom to tell him the truth about her life.

She stopped thinking about it when he said, "You set the pace. I want to make sure you have your second orgasm, and maybe even a third."

She was past ready to find satisfaction, and she imagined he was, too. Slowly she raised herself up and then took him in. He gripped her buttocks and groaned with pleasure. That was exactly what she wanted to hear. Soon each moment was all about giving and receiving, sharing and loving. She welcomed him deeper and the expression on his face told her he was experiencing what she was.

As they were both caught in a tornado that swirled them toward satisfaction, Cassie didn't want this moment to end. She trembled as each new sensation electrified her. She felt his hands, which were holding her waist, grip her tighter. The buildup of pleasurable tension suddenly unwound in glorious sensations that skittered through her nerve endings, making her weak. Then to her surprise Nash moved inside of her again and then again, and her second orgasm made her gasp. She collapsed on top of him and he wrapped his arms around her. His heart was beating fast against hers.

When she could finally breathe almost normally again, she told him, "That was incredible."

"I told you there'd be a number two," he said with a grin.

She'd never felt closer to another human being, and she didn't know how to tell him that.

After more time just holding each other, Nash reminded her, "We didn't have that conversation we were going to have."

"Maybe later?" she asked. "I have to start decorating for Renata's party."

"Having sex with you could make me forget all about a party."

Having sex. Those were the words he'd used to describe their lovemaking. Because he was afraid to say more? Was she?

"That conversation," she said. "It could be complicated. We need to know where we stand, Nash. We need to know what we're doing."

He frowned, but then he tipped her chin up to him and he kissed her. Afterward he asked, "Can't we just take one day at a time?"

Could they? Could she love him and then let him leave? Could she love him if he didn't love her?

But as he kissed her again, she knew she could because she was grateful for what they had right now. Still, a little voice in her head asked, *How will you feel when he leaves?*

She didn't have any answers and she knew she wasn't going to search for them now.

Chapter Thirteen

Several neighbors brought casseroles and desserts to the party that evening. They were sitting in the lounge area when Nash arrived. He spotted Cassie at the counter placing candles on a sheet cake decorated in pink, white and lime green icing. As her gaze met his, it was as if the whole room lit up for him. Suddenly he realized the older women gathered in the sitting area, friends of Renata's, he supposed, were watching him with curiosity.

Renata, who was sitting in the wing chair in the place of honor, told everyone else loud enough for Nash to hear, "He's Cassie's guest, but he's sweet on her, too."

Cassie had heard and she glanced at Nash, probably to see if he minded that characterization.

He sent her a crooked grin. "What are you going to do?" he asked. "It's not something I can hide easily." Crossing to her at the counter, he ran his finger along the edge of the cake resulting in a glob of icing on the tip.

Cassie teasingly slapped his arm. "What are you doing?"

He wiggled his brows. "I'm just making sure the icing is five-star." He tasted some of it, then with a wink held his finger to her lips. After only a brief hesitation, she licked it. The sensuality of her tongue on his skin heated his blood like a flash fire.

He leaned close to her and murmured, "Maybe after everyone leaves tonight, we could share a piece of cake with icing."

She fanned herself with her hand. "It's hot in here, don't you think?"

He laughed. "I'll take that as a *yes*."

Turning away, Cassie picked up the pack of matches and lit the candles. She asked Nash, "Do you want to do the honors? I think Renata will appreciate it. She's sweet on you, too."

Without a comment, Nash carried the cake out to the guest of honor. Then he took out his cell phone and took a photo as everyone in the room sang "Happy Birthday" and Renata blew out the candles.

She was smiling broadly as she said, "Thank you so much for tonight. I feel special."

Cassie went over to the wing chair and crouched down beside her. "You *are* special." After she kissed Renata on the cheek, she stood and picked up the cake knife that she'd laid on the coffee table. "Now, who wants a piece of cake?"

There was a chorus of "I shouldn't, but I will."

Just as Cassie was flipping the first slice onto a dish, Nash's cell phone buzzed. The caller was Ben Fortune.

"I have to take this," he said to Cassie.

She nodded. "I'll be busy serving and they'll be busy eating. Go ahead. I'll save you a piece of cake."

Her face was upturned, her eyes were bright and her smile full of joy. Nash just wanted to kiss her. Not *just* kiss her. He'd have liked to take her back to her bedroom right now. But that would have to wait until the party was over.

He went to the farthest corner of the kitchen to take the call. "Tremont here."

"Nash, it's Ben."

It was still hard for him to think of Ben as his half brother. He wasn't sure if he wanted to or not.

"Still trying to make up your mind about us?" Ben asked.

"Something like that. How can I help you?"

"Keaton and I would like you to meet more of your Fortune half siblings. Maybe then you'll tell us the information you're looking for and maybe we can give it to you. What do you say?"

What would he be stepping into if he said yes? His cover was already blown. Was this the only way to get more information?

Since he'd met Keaton and Ben, he was wondering about the rest of his family and what they'd be like. Did he want to meet "family"?

Whatever the reason, he found himself answering, "All right. I'll meet more of them. But under one condition."

"What's that?" Ben inquired.

"I want to make it perfectly clear that I do *not* want to see or meet Gerald…at least not for now."

"I can make sure Gerald has nothing to do with this meeting. It may take me a little time to set it up, but I'll get back to you with the time and place."

"I'll be leaving in a week."

"I'll keep that in mind," Ben said. "You won't be sorry you're doing this."

But as Nash said goodbye and ended the call, he wasn't sure whether he'd be sorry or not. Did he still want to go after Charlotte? Maybe he would wait until after the meeting and then decide.

When Cassie awakened, she'd never felt happier. She was facing Nash, her arm around his waist, his arm around her. She'd slept tucked into his shoulder almost all night. *Almost* because they'd made love instead of talking after the party, then had made love again when they'd both awakened a few hours later. Cassie realized she should feel tired but she didn't. She felt energized and invigorated.

She must have made some tiny movement—she loved rubbing her thumb along Nash's skin—because his eyes opened and he studied her. "How long have you been awake?"

"Not long." With only a few inches between them, he didn't have to move much to kiss her. And once he was kissing her, they were entwined again, ready to start all over to climb the pleasure mountain they'd scaled more than once last night.

Cassie was totally unprepared for the sound of her phone ringing on the nightstand beside Nash.

On top of her, Nash looked down and asked, "Do you always get calls this early in the morning?"

"It's really not that early," she said, checking the clock beside her. "I should be starting breakfast. It's after seven."

Since her cordless landline phone was on Nash's side of the bed, he picked it up and in a professional voice said, "This is the Bluebonnet Bed-and-Breakfast. How can I help you?"

Cassie jabbed him in the ribs, but waited to see how he'd handle the call. If someone wanted to make a reservation, maybe he'd do a good job of it.

Soon she could see that the caller didn't want to make a reservation. Suddenly Nash was frowning and looking much too serious. He had a very stern look on his face when he passed her the phone. "She says she's your mother."

Her mother? Was this a joke? Cassie's mother hadn't wanted to speak to her or see her since she'd gone to jail. With trembling fingers Cassie took the phone in hand, staring at Nash, but thinking about her mom.

"Hello," she said tentatively.

"Cassie, it's your mom."

"I can't believe you finally called."

"I know, baby, and I only have a minute. I know I've been real stubborn about this, but there was a good reason. I've been getting counseling and I've finally gotten clean of my cravings. You know I was always good at tailoring and sewing. I'm studying fashion design. I just wanted you to know that."

Cassie swallowed hard and glanced at Nash again. His features were stoic.

Years ago her mom had made her clothes...when she

wasn't drunk. Was her mother really on the road to recovery? She asked, "Can I visit you?"

"Not yet. But I'll call you soon and give you another progress report. I promise. I want to make sure I'm strong and ready to be a proper mother when I get out."

If her mother wasn't drinking, maybe she'd keep her promise. "It's good to hear from you," Cassie assured her mom, her voice catching and tears coming to her eyes. "Call me whenever you want. Do you have my cell number?"

"I do. It's on my approved list of contacts. You take care of yourself, baby. I have to go."

Her mother clicked off and Cassie suddenly felt as lost as she had when her mother had gone to jail.

And now…now she had to face Nash.

Nash had gotten up and dressed. He sat on the bedroom chair, his gaze piercing as it targeted her. She imagined his expression was similar to when he questioned a witness in one of his investigations. She knew he wanted some sort of explanation. Just how was she going to explain this?

Instead of trying, she said, "It's complicated." He'd once told her that about *his* situation.

Apparently that wasn't enough for Nash and she hadn't expected it would be. But her response had bought her enough time to take a deep breath.

"That was your mother?" he asked.

How could she put all of her story into words? Moreover, how could she say she'd been afraid to tell him?

Nash's reaction to her silence wasn't patience. As if he wasn't willing to wait for her to find the right words, he asked, "What the hell is going on?" Anger was evident in his tone.

Feeling self-conscious, Cassie tugged the sheet up over her breasts. She didn't want to feel any more vulnerable before him right now. She felt too shaky, too exposed, too naked.

Finally, she raised her gaze to his and didn't flinch when his brown eyes locked to hers. "My mother is alive. She's living in Travis State Prison."

Nash looked as if someone had sucker punched him in the solar plexus. "Did I hear you right? Your mother is in prison?"

Cassie nodded, unable to explain further since her throat was tightening, her chest was seizing and tears were burning her eyes.

He stood. "You didn't think I'd want to know this?"

Before Cassie could find any more words, before she could even think about where she wanted to begin, Nash pulled his car keys from his pocket. "I have to go."

Her throat was so tight, her heart so panicked, that he'd left before she could pull herself together enough to get dressed. Not knowing what else to do, she dragged the sheet around her to the doorway of her room. But when she got there, she heard the bang of the front door. He was gone and she didn't know when she was going to see him again…if ever.

Cassie worried all day, not just about her own feelings or about her mother. She worried about Nash. She thought maybe he'd call or stop back in. But he didn't do either. At one point in the afternoon she couldn't stand the waiting. She took fresh towels into his room and saw that his laptop was still there along with a briefcase. He certainly wouldn't go back to Biloxi without them.

She checked in guests around four o'clock—a businessman and a cowgirl who was following the rodeo circuit. They both signed up for supper, so Cassie made a dinner any traveler would enjoy. As she planned it, she knew that if Nash came back for supper, he'd like what she made. She served the fried chicken and mashed potato dinner family style with cranberry-orange salad and a steamed veggie mix. Dessert was easy enough—chocolate cupcakes with chocolate icing.

But even cooking couldn't keep her mind off Nash. He wasn't back at the Bluebonnet by seven...or even by eleven. By one in the morning, Cassie was more than frazzled. She was panicked and sick at heart. She prayed that nothing had happened to him. She'd tried dialing his phone number over and over, but he wasn't answering. Her messages asking him to call seemed to become more desperate and she hated that about them.

She rose early the next morning and mixed a batch of cinnamon rolls. While the dough was rising, she found Nash's registration form in her file and called his friend's number.

Dave Preston answered with a laugh. "What's the matter, Nash? Did you lose your cell phone?"

Cassie was calling from the landline and she knew Dave Preston had seen the ID—Bluebonnet Bed-and-Breakfast.

"No, Mr. Preston, this is Cassie Calloway at the Bluebonnet."

"Something hasn't happened to Nash, has it?" Dave asked, obviously concerned.

"There hasn't been an accident or anything like that."

"That's a relief. But why are you calling? Further references?"

"No. But I'm worried about him. We had a...fight

of sorts and he didn't come back last night. I have no idea where he might be and I'm worried sick. I thought maybe if *you* tried to call him, he'd answer."

"I see," Dave said.

"I just need to know that he's okay. I need to talk to him, but if he doesn't want to talk to me, tell him I'll understand."

"I want to make sure *I* understand this," Dave responded. "Nash has become more than a guest at your bed-and-breakfast?"

"Yes, he has. We've become quite close over the last few weeks. But there's been a misunderstanding and I want to be able to explain to him why I...why I wasn't completely honest with him."

She heard Dave sigh. "Nash believes there's honesty and then there are lies. He calls it like he sees it."

She didn't need to be told that. "Can you see if you can get in touch with him?"

"I'll try. Do you have a number I can text you if I do reach him? I don't want to get in the middle of this, but you deserve to know if he's okay."

She rattled off her cell number, then added, "Thank you."

"No thanks necessary. I'll be in touch."

When Cassie replaced the handset on its base, she at least felt less alone. Dave Preston sounded as if he really cared for Nash. If that was the case, she'd just have to wait for his text.

When Nash's cell phone buzzed, he was just coming awake after lying atop the spread in a two-bit hotel for the night. He knew his phone couldn't have much battery left. His charger was still back at the B&B along with his laptop and the rest of his things. He was going to have to go collect them this morning whether he wanted to see Cassie or not.

Could she be trying to call again? Did he care if she was? His heart hurt just thinking about it.

Taking the phone off the nightstand, he saw Dave was calling him. "What's up?" he asked his friend.

"The bigger question is—are *you* still alive?" Dave asked with some sarcasm.

"Since I answered the call, I guess I am," Nash retorted.

"Well, that's good to know because now I have to text Cassie and tell her you're still kicking."

"Cassie? What do you have to do with Cassie?"

"Apparently she's worried about your hide. Apparently she dug out my number and called me. She asked me if I could find you because you weren't answering her calls. Is that true?"

Nash puffed up his pillow behind him and closed his eyes. "Yeah, it's true."

"Do you want to tell me why?"

"No, I don't."

"Do it anyway because now I'm in the middle of this."

"What did she tell you?"

"Not enough, and I'm tired of playing twenty questions. What's going on, Nash?"

"She lied to me."

There was a beat of silence before Dave asked, "What about?"

"I was under the impression her parents were dead. That's what her neighbor told me. But it turns out that's not true. Cassie just let me believe it because her mother's in prison."

"Whoa."

"That's all you have to say?"

"I have a lot more to say but you probably don't want to hear it."

Nash groaned. "I know that won't stop you."

"You're right. Just let me put a scenario in front of you. Just say, you fall in love with a detective."

Nash was about to cut in, but Dave stopped him. "Let me finish. You fall in love with a detective. You aren't one in this case. However, your father was locked up in jail for God knows what crime, and you were afraid you'd lose her if you told her."

Shifting restlessly on the bed, Nash was uncomfortable with Dave's example. "If I loved her, I'd have to eventually tell her."

"Yes, that's true. But how much time is enough time? And how deeply in love do you have to be before the person you love can handle the truth?"

Nash didn't have an answer to that. "My phone's ready to cut out. I don't have my charger."

"Isn't that such a good excuse not to listen to me? Think about what I said, Nash, and then go talk to Cassie. I know Sara hurt you. But don't use this as a barrier to keep from feeling again. I'll text Cassie that you're still alive."

The screen on Nash's phone went black. It matched his mood exactly. He had to go back to the B&B for his things, so he might as well talk to Cassie if she was there. If she wasn't, he'd be on his way back to Biloxi. After he returned to Mississippi, he'd give Ben Fortune a call. If a meeting was going to take place with other half siblings, he'd drive back here again for it. That just didn't seem as important as it had been. Neither did his investigation.

He didn't even want to think about that right now. His mind was buzzing with what he'd say to Cassie if he saw her.

A half hour later, he was climbing the steps to the B&B when a man and a woman came out. They were talking to each other. The man said, "That's the best breakfast I've had in a long time."

"Cassie certainly knows how to cook. I'm looking forward to tonight's meal. Are you going to be there?"

"I am. I'll catch you then."

The man and woman went their separate ways.

Yes, Cassie did know how to cook. He was trying to forget about that as well as her smile, the way her eyes lit up when she was excited and the sound of her laughter.

As soon as he walked into the B&B, he sensed Cassie's presence. She was cleaning up the kitchen.

He couldn't help but notice that she looked pale and there were blue half-moons under her eyes. Had she been up most of the night worrying about him? He felt guilty and, along with the love he knew he felt for her, he knew he never wanted to hurt her again. But what was she feeling right now?

When her gaze met his, he approached the counter. Because of all the emotion he was feeling, his voice was gruff when he asked, "Did Dave text you?"

"Yes, he did. Thank him for me, will you?"

Nash gave her a nod before saying, "I came to re-trieve my things."

Her eyes widened and glistened with sudden emotion. As she came from around the counter, he stepped back.

"You're being unfair," she accused.

Maybe he'd known that before he walked in the door. Still, he became defensive because she had lied to him. Because he hurt so badly thinking about going home, because he wanted to kiss her more than he wanted to breathe, he returned, "What kind of relationship could we have if you can't be honest with me?" He held his breath while he waited for her answer.

"Will you at least hear me out?" she pleaded.

She looked so doggone pretty in a hot-pink T-shirt and some sort of shorts that looked like a skirt. She was even in her bare feet.

He crossed his arms over his chest. "I'm listening."

She sat on one of the stools as if her legs were shaking and wouldn't hold her up anymore. She faced him. "When I moved here and bought the B&B, I told people my mom had died and so had my dad. That was easier than trying to explain the situation and having to endure looks of pity or horror. Even worse than those was the judgment that went along with knowing my mom was in prison. That relationship I told you about that the guy broke off? He did that when I explained my mother was in prison." She didn't give him a chance to speak, drawing a breath and accusing, "You kept secrets, too. Why are mine so much worse than yours?"

Secrets? Yes, he'd had secrets. But he'd told her all about them. Why couldn't she have told him? The question ate at him. He skirted the issue and asked, "What did your mother want?"

Tears came to Cassie's eyes now and one rolled

down her cheek. He felt his chest tighten and his fingers clench.

"My mother was and is an alcoholic. In my last year of college, she was driving drunk and hit another car. The man died. She was charged with vehicular homicide."

"What did you do?" Nash asked.

"I was on my own. My high school art teacher and I had stayed in touch. When she learned I had to move out of our rented apartment, she let me stay with her. Between my scholarship and jobs, I was able to make it. But my mom… When she went to prison, she didn't want to see me or talk to me. She told me it was better for me that way. So in a way, it was like my mom *had* died. When she called yesterday…" Cassie's voice broke. "That was the first I've talked to her in years."

Although Nash wanted to go to Cassie, he didn't. "That whole experience had to be awful for you." Silence lay between them until he asked, "Why did your mom call?"

"She couldn't talk long, but she told me she's been getting counseling and she's not having cravings."

"What about your dad?" he asked. "Is he really dead?"

"I have no idea if he's alive or dead. He left when I was a toddler, and my mom never heard from him again. That's when she started drinking."

As he thought about everything Dave had said to him, he imagined himself in Cassie's shoes. No communication with her mother and no dad. He understood the "no dad" part from personal experience. In his police work he'd seen families broken apart by alcoholism, and he could only imagine what Cassie had experienced. Did he want her to tell him? Would she?

"I'm going to go upstairs," he began.

"You're leaving?" She looked stricken.

"No. I'm going to get a shower while you make another pot of coffee. Then I'll be down and we can talk. Okay with you?"

She was crying openly now and she nodded.

Nash climbed the stairs, trying to figure out if following his heart was the foolish thing...or the smart thing to do.

When Cassie had received Dave's text that Nash was okay, she'd practically collapsed with relief. And now? She didn't know what was going to happen next. After they talked, Nash would probably leave. Maybe he just didn't want to leave on a sour note.

She'd just poured two mugs of coffee when Nash descended the stairs. He looked so good in a cream T-shirt and blue jeans. But she had to steel her heart against what he might say.

She couldn't read anything from his expression when he picked up both the mugs and nodded to the sofa. "Let's go over there and talk."

She followed him and sat on the sofa first. To her surprise, he sat right beside her...so close that their legs were touching.

He took both of her hands in his. "I *have* been unfair to you, Cassie. None of what happened to you was your fault. You had to cope with it as best you could. I think we both have some trust issues to work through. I've done a lot of thinking in the last twelve hours since Dave called me. He helped me look at your story differently. Can you forgive me for saying what I did...for leaving like that and not taking your calls?"

Obviously, Nash wanted the truth so she had to tell him the truth. "Yes, I can forgive you. But I have to ask—will you bolt again at the first sign of trouble between us?"

Gazing directly into her eyes now, he revealed, "No, I won't bolt. Because I realized last night that I love you. I fell hard and fast, though I couldn't admit it to myself, let alone you. That's why it hurt so bad when you didn't tell me about your parents. But I won't deny my feelings again, because they're too important. Love doesn't come around every day. I believe in vows and getting married in a church and swearing before God and everyone that we'll be committed to each other for a lifetime. Will you marry me?"

Cassie was shocked and surprised at Nash's question. Relief poured through her. She gazed at him with all the love she was feeling. "I promise I'll never keep anything from you again. Yes, I'll marry you. Would you want me to move to Biloxi? Do you want me to sell the B&B?"

He was shaking his head. "I don't want you to sell the B&B. You love it here. And Biloxi? Biloxi was just a stopping-over point for me. I'm going to look into jobs in Austin, either with the police force or with a private security company. But I do think we'll have to buy a double bed for your suite. We'll take our time. We'll get engaged. We'll really get to know each other."

"Will my mother be a stumbling block for you when she gets out of prison?"

"Your mom gave you the gift of life. You've turned out to be a wonderful person, so she can't be all bad, right? I know you think I see things in black-and-white, and that's why you couldn't tell me. But the truth is, since I met you, I see a whole spectrum of colors. We'll deal with your mom and anything else we have to deal with. I love you that much, Cassie."

Cassie took Nash's face between her hands. "I love you, Nash Tremont." Her voice was so joyous and her smile so radiant she knew Nash couldn't have a doubt about her feelings.

When he took her into his arms to kiss her, a kiss that spoke of love and forgiveness and promise, she knew she was exactly where she was supposed to be.

After they were both breathless from the kiss, he scooped her up in his arms to carry her to her bedroom. "Do you think you can get away for a few days?" he asked her.

"I suppose I can," she answered. "Reservations are spotty. I can easily block out a few days. Why?"

"Because I want to take you to Oklahoma to meet my mother."

Cassie had never been this happy, not in her entire life. She kissed Nash's neck and held on to him tighter. Then he carried her into her suite—their suite now—and closed the door.

Epilogue

It was late morning a few days later when Cassie looked around her suite to see what she could do to make it suitable for her *and* Nash. She'd jotted down a few ideas and she was adding to those when she heard the front door to the B&B open and close…and the sound of boots.

Nash was back.

She stuck her head outside the doorway and called to him. "In here."

She couldn't tell anything from his expression as he met her in the doorway.

He saw the clipboard in her hands and raised his brows. "What are you doing?"

"I'm redecorating. But I can tell you that later. How did it go with your appointments this morning?"

"There's a good chance that I'll be part of the Austin PD. I'm set up for an interview tomorrow. Of course, they'll have to do all the background paperwork. One of their homicide detectives retired and they need somebody to fill the spot."

"Homicide?" Cassie asked.

"Does it scare you if I quit white-collar crimes and become a homicide detective? I can probably find a job in private security if it does. I sent a few résumés last night to companies in Austin. We could see which job pans out first."

Cassie knew what had happened in Nash's last relationship...why he would do what *she* wanted, rather than what *he* wanted. But that wasn't the way they were going to live their lives.

She took his face between her hands and looked straight into his eyes. "I want you to do the work that will fulfill you and satisfy you. That's what matters to me. If you're a homicide detective, I'll trust you to make the right decisions to keep yourself safe. If you want to work for private security, that's fine with me, too."

He gathered her into his arms and gave her a long, deep kiss.

When she broke away, she told him, "Besides painting the room a color you'd like, I thought we could get rid of the love seat and chair and put in a double bed. We might still have room for the chair."

"A double bed, huh?" he asked with a sexy grin. I don't think we'll need the chair as long as we have the bed."

She laughed, stepped away and then became serious again. "I have a question to ask you."

"Go ahead."

"My mother said she'd call again soon. When she does, I'm going to ask her if she'll let me visit her."

"All right," Nash said.

"I'd like to ask her to put your name on the visitors list, too. I want to tell her about *us* and I'd like you to meet her." Cassie studied Nash's face—the lines she was beginning to know so well, the jut sometimes of his stubborn jaw. Still, she couldn't tell exactly what he was thinking.

Not until he said, "I'd like to meet your mother... without judgment. Just face value. Then we'll go from there."

She threw her arms around him again. "Thank you!"

"I have a question for you, too."

"Ask," she said, ready to tell him anything he wanted to know.

Before she could realize what he was doing, he'd stepped away and he'd gotten down on one knee. Out of his pocket, he pulled a little black velvet box. When he opened it, she saw a beautiful antique ring of diamonds in white gold. She was speechless.

"I went to a jeweler who sells estate jewelry. I wanted something unique for you," Nash explained. "So I'm going to ask you again to make our engagement official. Will you marry me, Cassie Calloway, and spend the rest of your life with me? We can have a short engagement or a long engagement. But I want to know we're committed to each other."

"I'm committed to you," Cassie said seriously. "And, yes, I'll marry you...any time, any place...any how."

Nash took the ring from the box and slipped it onto her finger. Then he rose to his feet.

After he kissed her again, he murmured close to her ear, "I kind of like your single bed. Maybe we should use it as much as we can before we get the double." With his booted foot, he pushed the door closed, then scooped her up in his arms and carried her to the bed.

Cassie had no doubt that their trust would grow each day…just as would their commitment and their love.

* * * * *

*Don't miss the next installment of the new
Harlequin Special Edition continuity*
**THE FORTUNES OF TEXAS:
THE RULEBREAKERS**

*When Maddie Fortunado's secret crush,
Zach McCarter, becomes the obstacle standing
between her and her professional dreams, she knows
she has to step up her game. Her first step?
A makeover guaranteed to change the girl next
door into a heartbreaker...but will love complicate
her plans?*

Look for
MADDIE FORTUNE'S PERFECT MAN
by
Nancy Robards Thompson

And catch up with the Fortune family by reading
HER SOLDIER OF FORTUNE
by Michelle Major

NO ORDINARY FORTUNE
by USA TODAY Bestselling Author Judy Duarte

THE FORTUNE MOST LIKELY TO...
*by USA TODAY Bestselling Author
Marie Ferrarella*

*Available now, wherever Harlequin books
and ebooks are sold.*

#2617 THE NANNY'S DOUBLE TROUBLE
The Bravos of Valentine Bay • by Christine Rimmer
Despite their family connection, Keely Ostergard and Daniel Bravo have never gotten along. But when Keely steps in as emergency nanny to Daniel's twin toddlers, she quickly finds herself sweet on the single dad.

#2618 MADDIE FORTUNE'S PERFECT MAN
The Fortunes of Texas: The Rulebreakers
by Nancy Robards Thompson
When Maddie Fortunado's father announces that she and Zach McCarter—Maddie's secret office crush—are competing to be his successor, Maddie's furious. But as they work together to land a high-profile listing, they discover an undeniable chemistry and a connection that might just pull each of them out of the fortifications they've built to protect their hearts.

#2619 A BACHELOR, A BOSS AND A BABY
Conard County: The Next Generation • by Rachel Lee
Diane Finch is fostering her cousin's baby and can't find suitable day care. In steps her boss, Blaine Harrigan, who loves kids and just wants to help. As they grow closer, will the secret Diane is keeping be the thing that tears them apart?

#2620 HER WICKHAM FALLS SEAL
Wickham Falls Weddings • by Rochelle Alers
Teacher Taryn Robinson leaves behind a messy breakup and moves to a small town to become former navy SEAL Aiden Gibson's young daughters' tutor. Little does she know she's found much more than a job—she's found a family!

#2621 THE LIEUTENANTS' ONLINE LOVE
American Heroes • by Caro Carson
Thane Carter and Chloe Michaels are both lieutenants in the same army platoon—and they butt heads constantly. Luckily, they have their online pen pals to vent to. Until Thane finds out the woman he's starting to fall for is none other than the workplace rival he's forbidden to date!

#2622 REUNITED WITH THE SHERIFF
The Delaneys of Sandpiper Beach • by Lynne Marshall
Shelby and Conor promised to meet on the beach two years after the best summer of their lives, but when Shelby never showed, Conor's heart was shattered. Now she's back in Sandpiper Beach and working at his family's hotel. Can Conor let the past go long enough to see if they can finally find forever?

Get 2 Free Books,

Plus 2 Free Gifts—

just for trying the Reader Service!

But Thane took only one more step before stopping, watching
in horror as Michaels entered row D from the other side.
Good God, what were the odds? This was ridiculous. It was
the biggest night of his life, the night when he was finally
going to meet the woman of his dreams, and Michaels was
here to make it all difficult.

He retreated. He backed out of the row and went back up
a few steps, row E, row F, going upstream against the flow of
people. He paused there. He'd let Michaels take her seat, then
he'd go back in and be careful not to look toward her end of
the row as he took his seat in the center. If he didn't make eye
contact, he wouldn't have to acknowledge her existence at all.

He watched Michaels pass seat after seat after seat, smiling
and nodding thanks as she worked her way into the row, his
horror growing as she got closer and closer to the center of
the row, right to where he and Ballerina were going to meet.